WEDDINGS
& WASABI

WEDDINGS & WASABI

Camy Tang

author of *Sushi for One?*

WinePressPublishing
Great Books, Defined.

WinePress Publishing (PO Box 428, Enumclaw, WA 98022) functions only as book publisher. As such, the ultimate design, content, editorial accuracy, and views expressed or implied in this work are those of the author.

The author of this book has waived a portion of the publisher's recommended professional editing services. As such, any related errors found in this finished product are not the responsibility of the publisher.

Unless otherwise noted, all Scriptures are taken from the *Holy Bible, New International Version*®, *NIV*®. Copyright © 1973, 1978, 1984 by Biblica, Inc.™ Used by permission of Zondervan. All rights reserved worldwide. www.zondervan.com

ISBN 13: 978-1-4141-2059-1
ISBN 10: 1-4141-2059-1
Library of Congress Catalog Card Number: 2011924148

To every single person who emailed,
Tweeted, or Facebooked me
asking for Jenn's story.
Here it is.

ACKNOWLEDGMENTS

THIS BOOK WOULD not exist without Audra Harder's help with the goats. I'm totally serious when I say that.

Thanks also to my ex-roommates from our Palo Alto house: Cathy, Chrissy, Mary, Eileen, Elaine, Linda, and Soojin. You guys will recognize the strangely familiar scene in Aunty Aikiko's house. The names have been changed to protect the not-so-innocent.

CHAPTER ONE

THE GOAT IN the backyard had just eaten tonight's dinner.

Jennifer Lim stood on her mother's miniscule back porch and glared at the small brown-and-white creature polishing off her basil. She would have run shouting at it to leave off her herb garden, except it had already decimated the oregano, mint, rosemary, thyme, cilantro, and her precious basil, which had been slated for tonight's pesto.

Besides, if it bit her, she was peeved enough to bite back.

"Mom!" She stomped back into the house. Thank goodness the pots of her special Malaysian basil were sectioned off in the large garden on the side of the house, protected by a wooden-framed wire gate. Jenn was growing it so she could make her cousin Trish's favorite chicken dish for her wedding, which Jenn was catering for her. But everything in her backyard garden was gone. The animal was welcome to the only thing left, the ragged juniper bushes. Were juniper bushes poisonous? If so, the animal was welcome to them.

"Mom!" Her voice had reached banshee range. "There is a goat—"

"You don't need to yell." Mom entered the kitchen, her lipstick bright red from a fresh application and her leather handbag over her arm, obviously ready to leave the house on some errand.

I

"Since when do we own a goat?"

"Since your cousin Larry brought him over." She fished through her leather purse. "His name is Pookie."

Jenn choked on her demand for an explanation, momentarily distracted. "He has a name?"

"He's a living being. Of course he has a name." Her mother fluttered eyelashes overloaded with mascara.

"Don't give me that. You used to love to gross me out with stories of Great-Uncle Hao Chin eating goats back in China."

Mom sniffed and found the refrigerator fascinating. "That's your father's side."

Jenn swayed as the floor tilted. *You are now entering ... the Twilight Zone.* Her one remaining parent had evoked that feeling quite often in the past few weeks. "Where did Larry get a goat, and why do we have it now?"

"They were desperate."

Actually, Jenn could have answered her own question. That goat was in their backyard right now because everyone knew that her mom couldn't say no to a termite who knocked on the door and asked if it could spend the night.

And outside of physically dropping the goat off at someone's house—and she didn't have an animal trailer, so that was out of the question—Jenn wouldn't be able to get anyone else in the family to agree to take the animal, now that it was here. That meant leaving a goat in a niece's backyard because no one else wanted to go through the hassle of doing anything about it.

Mom said, "You wouldn't have me turn away family, would you?"

"Uncle Percy knows, too?"

"No, not Percy."

"Aunty Glenda?" No way. Even if Larry were eighty instead of eighteen, Aunty would still dictate to her son the color underwear he wore that day—how much more his choice of pet?

"No." Mom blinked as rapidly as she could with mascara making her short, stiff lashes stick together, almost gluing her eyes shut.

The tiger in Jenn's ribcage growled. "Mother." Her fist smacked onto her hip.

"Oh, all right." Mom rolled her eyes as if she were still a teenager. "It belongs to Larry's dormmate's older brother, but really, he's the nicest young man." Burgundy lips pulled into what wanted to be a smile but instead looked hideously desperate.

Jenn tried to count to ten but only got to two. "I know Larry's a nice young man. If an abundance of immaturity counts as 'nice' points."

"Jenn, really, you're so intolerant. Just because you're smart and went to Stanford for grad school ..."

The name of her school—and the one dominant memory it brought up—made her neck jerk in a spasm. It had only been for two years, but that was enough. Desperately lonely after spending her undergrad years living with her cousins, Jenn had only formed a few friendships among the other grad students, none of them close. There was only one person she'd never forget, although every morning when she got up and saw the scar in the mirror, she desperately wanted to erase him from her memory.

"Why. Do we have. A goat."

"It's only for a few days—"

"We don't know a thing about how to take care of—"

"They're easy—"

"Besides which, this is Cupertino. I'm sure there are city laws—"

"It'll be gone before anyone notices—"

"Oh, ho, you're right about that." Jenn strode toward the phone on the wall. "I'm calling the Humane Society. They'll take it." Although they wouldn't provide a trailer to transport it. How was she going to take the goat *anywhere*, much less to an animal shelter?

Mom plopped onto a stool and sighed. "That boy was so cute. His name was Brad."

There went her neck spasming again. But Brad was a common name. She grabbed the phone.

3

"Such a nice Chinese boy. Related to the Yip family—you know, the ones in Mountain View?"

The phone slipped from her hand and bungee jumped toward the floor, saved only by the curly cord. She bent to snatch it up, but dizziness shrouded her vision, and she had to take a few breaths before straightening up.

"Oh, and he went to Stanford. You two have something in common." Mom beamed.

No. He wouldn't.

Yes, he would.

"Brad Yip?"

Mom's eyes lighted up. "Do you know him?"

Sure, she knew him. Knew the next time he came for his goat she'd ram her chef's knife, Michael Meyers style, right between his eyes.

CHAPTER TWO

WHAT SHOULD HAVE been a joyous party celebrating her culinary degree had turned horrible. Like finding a cockroach in her bowl of soup.

The "cockroach" in question stood a head taller than Jenn's relatives, doing that male head-nod-sip-drink-laugh that indicated "bonding" as they watched a few of the younger kids battling it out on the Wii. His smile had once made her stomach flop. It still did, but this time to cast up the makuzushi she'd just eaten, the vinegar rice from the sushi burning the back of her throat. Her glare should have clawed that relaxed smile off his deceitful face.

Venus followed Jenn's gaze. "Who's the guy you're stabbing with your eyes?"

"The scum of the earth."

Venus's eyebrows arched as she turned to Jenn.

"That's *him*." Jenn fingered the scar on her cheek.

Her cousin's eyes suddenly burned like charcoal. "You're kidding. Who brought him?"

"I don't know." The conversation yesterday filtered through her raging thoughts. "Maybe Larry."

"Larry? How would he know him?"

"Larry's apparently dorming with Brad's younger brother."

Venus's poise faltered far enough for her to drop her jaw. "I don't believe it. What are the odds?"

Jenn didn't answer, just glowered at him.

Venus's eyes narrowed slightly. "And how do you know all this?"

"Because he foisted his goat on my mother yesterday."

Venus blinked. "Come again?"

"I wasn't home. Larry brought Brad to Mom yesterday, and they asked her to take Brad's goat."

"His goat? Why does he own a goat?"

Jenn threw her hands up. "Why don't you ask him?"

Venus's brow fell, and she gave a short motion with her hands. "Chill."

Jenn bit her lip. "Sorry."

Venus frowned at Brad as he and their cousins laughed loudly. "Why in the world did he come to your party? What nerve."

How could he just stand there? Having a good time? As if what he'd done to her hadn't happened?

No, she wasn't going to be a victim ever again. Steel shot through her veins, straightening her shoulders. "I'm going to ask him."

Venus grabbed her arm. "What?"

Jenn shook off her hand and moved forward. "I'm going to ask him."

Venus caught her elbow again. "No, you're not."

"Why?" She tried to pull away, but Venus's fingers tightened.

"You shouldn't have to." Venus scanned the room. "Where's Lex?"

"That hurts." She knocked Venus's hand away. "You can't keep protecting me—"

A suffocating cloud of lilac preceded Aunt Aikiko, then smothered Jenn as Aunty gave her a hug. "Congratulations on your graduation!"

Jenn coughed. "Thanks, Aunty."

CHAPTER TWO

"I'm so proud of you." Aunty beamed at her, still keeping her hands at Jenn's shoulders. "It took you so long, but you finally got your certificate."

Jenn damped down her irritation. "Thanks, Aunty. Actually, it's not a certificate, it's an Associate of Occupational Studies degree—"

"And now you can work in my restaurant." Aunty's expression was a mix of self-congratulations for acquiring family labor and an invisible push at her niece to walk the line of her plans.

But perversely, Jenn stiffened.

Now why would she do that? Probably because of Brad's grating voice filtering through the party noise. Her tight jaw wouldn't let her smile, so instead, she nodded.

Venus didn't say anything, but she crossed her arms and turned away slightly. She'd probably bring up their old argument as soon as Aunty walked away, and Jenn was too dispirited to rehash all the reasons why she was going to work at Aunty's *okazuya* in Japantown. Plus she was tired of Venus and Lex always trying to protect her. She was thirty-three, not thirteen. "Aunty, did you have the crab puffs? It's a new recipe I'm trying."

She tried to steer her toward the buffet table, but Uncle Howard came up and hugged her hard, his hand slapping her shoulder blades. "Jenn, my favorite niece with a culinary degree."

Jenn resisted rolling her eyes at the old joke. "Uncle, I'm your only niece with a culinary degree."

"So are you going to use that degree and work for your aunty?"

Aunty Aikiko simpered.

"Um ... of course." So why did she feel like a fish in a net? Hadn't she taken culinary management classes specifically because Aunty had hinted that she wanted Jenn to take over the restaurant one day? Aunty and her husband, Uncle Aki, must be good managers—the small restaurant had grown by leaps and bounds—so Jenn would learn a lot from them.

The problem was that Jenn didn't really want their Japanese restaurant. She wanted her own.

However, she hadn't voiced that desire to anyone because it almost seemed as if she'd jinx it if she did. Not to mention the fact that Aunty and all the relatives would be seriously displeased if she ditched Aunty's restaurant to start her own, and Jenn wasn't quite willing to brave their censure … and crying and arguing and yelling and nagging (this was the Sakai family, after all). Lex or Venus might not care about that, but Jenn was the quiet cousin, the one who liked everyone to get along.

Uncle Howard pounded her back again. "We're all counting on you to help your aunty out."

The weight of his approval—of the entire family's approval and expectations—settled on her shoulders like a sandbag.

No, it was not a sandbag. She had to stop thinking negatively. It was a mantle.

That weighed fifty pounds.

Behind Uncle Howard, she could see Brad moving with her male cousins toward the back door of Grandma's house.

Venus took off after him. Even worse, she spied Lex standing with her husband, Aiden, and forcibly yanked her away from the conversation.

No way would Jenn let Venus "fix" things for her. Not with *him*. "Uncle, Aunty, I'm sorry, I need to talk to someone. Have some food." She scurried after Venus.

She had to dodge a few younger cousins running underfoot, and she almost trod on an old aunty's foot, but she caught up to her cousins just as Lex grabbed Brad's arm and jerked him aside.

"What are you doing here?" all three of them barked at once.

Brad, obviously still the egomaniac he'd always been, didn't seem fazed to be approached by three women. And being Brad, he also homed in on gorgeous Venus like a shark. "Hey, baby—"

"Stuff it, you rotten excuse for a human being," she snapped.

His dimples faded. "Uh …" His eye wandered to Lex without recognition, lingered on her slim form in a new silk blouse she (and Trish) had bought for Jenn's party.

CHAPTER TWO

Those eyes finally slid to Jenn. And then his arrogance reasserted itself in that slimy smile. "Oh, hi, Jenn. How are you doing?"

"How am I doing?" Her voice rose from its normal deep octave to one closer to the pitch only dogs can hear. "I was doing a lot better before I saw you here."

The insult washed over him. "Now, Jenn …" His tone was condescending.

"How dare you show your face here?" Lex fired at him.

"Mimi invited me." He glanced over his shoulder.

Their cousin, Aunty Aikiko's only daughter, had been chatting with a few of Trish's cousins on her mom's side, but Mimi now stopped and stared at them. Her face had whitened, but Jenn couldn't quite tell if she was angry at them for attacking her guest or shocked at their behavior, which, Jenn acknowledged, resembled semi-rabid dogs.

"How do you know Mimi?" Venus demanded.

A smile curled on his full lips. "We're dating."

"Dating?" all three cousins chorused.

How had they not known this? Well, then again, since Lex was no longer Mimi's housemate, they didn't keep up with their next youngest cousin as much as they used to. Jenn could believe that if their dating was a recent development, she and her cousins might not have heard about it yet through the Sakai family grapevine (which rivaled the World Wide Web for speed and exaggeration).

"What's going on?" Mimi came up to them, but Jenn noted with interest that she didn't do her normal proprietary slipping of her arm through her swain's.

Jenn had to choke through a burr in her throat. She blurted out, "This is the guy who hurt me in grad school."

Mimi's brow furrowed.

Venus's face looked stormy.

Lex's eyes shot darts at him.

9

Brad's faint smile never faltered. He sighed. "Jenn, you still haven't changed. Most children grow out of their make-believe stage, you know."

There was a beat of silence. Jenn had to snap shut her gaping mouth. She didn't want to bite at his dangling conversational hook, but something perverse and masochistic inside of her made her say, "What are you talking about?"

He looked puzzled. "Jenn, you're still telling everyone I hurt you, but you did it all to yourself, by yourself."

"You lying—" Lex looked like she was about to throw a punch, but Venus grabbed her wrist, hard, and she winced.

"I wasn't even in the room by then," he said, his calm demeanor still unperturbed.

"That's convenient," Jenn snarled. "Before, you said you were too drunk to remember much of anything."

"You were obviously too drunk to remember anything, either." There was a faint snicker in his tone.

Heat radiated up her neck and face as if she'd opened the door to an oven set on broil. She tried to tell herself his accusation was unfair. Since that night in grad school, she hadn't drunk alcohol other than a scant ounce of wine with dinner occasionally. But the memory of her wild behavior still felt like some hand twisting her guts around inside her.

"It's okay," he said with a fatherly smile. "We all overindulge once in a while. But you really should stop making up stories about what happened."

"You're the one making up stories. I have the scar to prove it."

"You fell into that bookcase by yourself—"

"I *fell?*" She was incredulous. "You're saying I happened to trip over hard enough to slam my face into that glass bowl, breaking it, and toppling your bookshelf? All by myself?"

He shrugged. "I don't know what happened after I left you passed out on the bed."

"You left me passed out on the floor, my cheek bleeding from the glass, while you and your friends went out partying." If her words were chef's knives, his throat would have been slashed.

He rolled his eyes. "Jenn, you told me to go with my friends. You were feeling sick. You laid down on my bed and told me to go away."

"That's it!" Lex shook off Venus's hand and shoved at Brad's shoulder with an angry finger. "You lying piece of—"

"She needed eight stitches," Venus spat. "Where were you?"

His eyes clouded with concern. "I didn't know that. I didn't know where you were."

"You mean the blood on your carpet didn't clue you in?" Jenn's vision started clouding in on the edges until all she saw were his lazy-lidded eyes and the red target between them where she wanted to plant her fist.

"I didn't even notice that until later—you know how messy I am." A rueful smile flashed over his mouth, then it firmed again in concern. "I'm really sorry. I didn't know what happened to you."

The innocent look on his face made her hesitate. What if he was right? What if she had been so drunk she had only imagined him pushing her into the bookshelf? What if she really had done that to herself?

No. She wasn't mistaken. "You were obviously so worried, you didn't call or e-mail me after that."

"Jenn, you don't even remember us breaking up just before I left the room."

It was true that she didn't remember him leaving her. She only remembered waking up in the empty room, her face in the sticky, blood-soaked carpet that smelled like copper and mold.

But she remembered enough. They hadn't broken up because she'd been unconscious. And yet he was spouting these lies with incredible calmness, making her look like a hysterical, delusional ex-girlfriend.

In front of all her family.

"Oh my goodness." Surprisingly, Venus's voice was calm, wondering, curious. "I've never met a real pathological liar before." She grabbed

Jenn by the arm and turned away from him. "Come on. No use arguing with the sociopath."

Was she serious? Jenn resisted.

But Lex took hold of her other arm, although with a firmer grip than Venus's. "Come on, before I do something I'll regret and end up in jail."

Jenn had a last fleeting look at Mimi, who stared at her with wide, burning eyes. Probably wondering if the real crazy person was the one walking away rather than the drop-dead gorgeous specimen of manhood standing next to her with admirable calm.

"I told you to press charges," Lex growled.

"After his family paid for my hospital bill? It would have been a slap in the face."

"You didn't ask them to do that. I told you before, I think they did it to keep you quiet—and it worked."

"And I told you, his family isn't exactly non-huge, non-powerful, non-rich, and non-famous in the Bay Area."

"Now, Lex," Venus said, still in that light, airy tone as if they had met an acquaintance for tea, "at the time she still loved Brad, even though he'd hurt her."

"What is up with you?" Lex glared at her over the top of Jenn's head.

"I'm fascinated. He's a bonafide sociopath, like that one *CSI: New York* episode guest starring ... what's her name? The girl from *The Secret Life of the American Teenager*? Shailene Woodley."

CSI? American Teenager? "What are you talking about?"

"Brad. He's kind of neat if you think about it."

"Venus!" Jenn stopped in her tracks and gaped at her. Maybe her cousin had lost it.

Venus opened her mouth to reply, but she didn't get a chance to—three aunties descended on the cousins like Greek Furies.

"Jennifer! How could you?" asked Great-Aunt Makiko, Grandma's youngest sister.

"You have completely embarrassed us all!" wailed Great-Aunt Mikiko, Grandma's second youngest sister.

"Just wait until your mother arrives!" threatened Aunty Meiko, Grandma's oldest daughter.

"Aunties, he's the one who caused this." Jenn pulled back her long hair, which she usually drew forward to cover the scar on her jawline.

The aunties hesitated, staring at the scar as if it were the first time they were seeing it. They probably hadn't seen it since that day years ago when she'd shown up with the stitches at a family birthday party she hadn't been able to escape attending.

"Pfft. That little thing?" Aunty Makiko said.

"I thought it was bigger than that," said Aunty Mikiko.

"You're making a fuss over that?" Aunty Meiko tagged along after her aunts' opinions.

Jenn's gut started boiling and burbling and foaming, steaming her head like a char siu bao. Lex had turned red and Venus had turned white.

The aunties continued. "He's Mimi's guest today."

"You should be nice to him."

"You're ruining Aunty Aikiko's party."

"Aunty's party?" Jenn exploded. "What are you talking about? This is a party to celebrate my getting my culinary degree."

"Of course it isn't." Aunty Makiko looked at her as if she were crazy.

"Jenn, really. You have to stop thinking only about yourself." Aunty Mikiko frowned at her.

"This party is to celebrate Uncle Aki's retiring, now that you'll be working for Aunty Aikiko at the restaurant, and also to introduce Mimi's new boyfriend to the family."

The ground seemed to be rumbling under Jenn's feet until she realized it was just her hands shaking in anger. "Uncle Aki's retirement? Mimi's new boyfriend?" She glanced back at Aunty Aikiko, who was talking to Brad and apparently trying to smooth the icing over the cracks their confrontation had caused in the party. Aunty Aikiko shot Jenn a malevolent look.

The aunties were chorusing. "Mimi never brings nice boys home."

"Aunty Aikiko was so happy she met Brad."

"He's from the Yip family. Did you know that?"

"Yes, I know that," Jenn snapped. "I used to date him."

"Of course Brad would look nice compared to Mimi's other boyfriends," Lex interjected. "He's not pierced, tattooed, or drunk."

"Or stoned," Venus added. "Or unemployed and living off his family."

"Really, girls," Aunty Makiko said. "That's not very nice."

"So don't you see why this is so exciting for Aunty Aikiko?" Aunty Mikiko said. "Mimi is her only daughter. Brad is such a catch."

"He hurt me!" Jenn burst out. "Doesn't that mean anything to any of you?"

Venus started. For good reason—Jenn couldn't remember the last time she'd spoken so disrespectfully to an aunty. But didn't they care about her? She was family. He was not.

"I'm sure he's grown out of his wild ways, and now he's very respectable," Aunty Meiko replied. "Why don't you give him a chance? He seems so friendly."

The emotions trembling through her suddenly stilled, like the eye of a storm. This was how it was, then. Years of doing her best to please them—including taking classes so she could eventually take over for Aunty Aikiko at the restaurant—all meant nothing.

She didn't mean anything to any of them. They didn't care about her. They couldn't care less about her.

Without even saying good-bye, Jenn turned from the three aunties and marched into the kitchen.

Venus and Lex hustled to keep up with her. "What are you doing?"

"I'm leaving."

"Your purse and coat are in the front room, not the kitchen," Lex said.

"I'll get them on the way out. If they don't want me here, then I'll leave—but I'm taking the food."

A wicked smile glinted in Venus's eyes.

They grabbed the plates of food Jenn had cooked and brought—for her graduation party, which apparently was not her own party after all—wrapping plates of cupcakes in foil to protect the artfully piped icing, sliding the baking pan of crab puffs back into the covered carrier, transferring the shrimp *shui mai* dumplings into their plastic container. While Jenn wrapped up the salt-and-pepper shrimp, Venus and Lex nipped out to the buffet table to grab the plates of food that had been moved out there, returning with half-eaten plates of deep-fried lobster balls and other appetizers.

"At least no one got the cupcakes yet," Lex muttered. "What a waste that would have been."

Venus whipped out her cell phone. "Trish called a few minutes ago to say she was on the way, but I'll tell her to meet us at Jenn's house instead. I'm sure you wouldn't want her to miss this spread."

Loaded with trays and Tupperware® containers, the three cousins headed toward the door, ignoring some curious looks from relatives. Jenn toed her shoes on and tried to free a hand so she could open the door. "Let's put the food in the car first, then come back for our coats and—"

The front door swung open. "Jenn!" her mother said. She sounded alarmed rather than just surprised to see her at the door.

A man stood beside her—Asian, older, with a moustache and a wide smile. "This is Jenn? How nice to meet you." He held a hand out to her but faltered when he saw her arms laden with food.

"Did you just get here?" Mom asked.

"No, I'm leaving." Jenn tried to shuffle a Tupperware®, but it almost fell to the floor.

"Oh." The man's face fell. "I was looking forward to chatting with you."

For some reason, Mom was avoiding Jenn's eyes.

Her grip tightened on the food carriers. "I'm sorry, do I know you?" He obviously knew who she was.

"I apologize. Here I am going on like this. Max Hiroyama." He wrapped his arm around Jenn's mom. "Your mother and I have been dating for a few weeks."

CHAPTER THREE

HOW COULD SHE not tell me?" Jenn stabbed a fork viciously into a shrimp *shu mai* steamed dumpling.

"No." Venus waved her chopsticks at Jenn, still holding onto her salt-and-pepper fried shrimp. "The real question is, how could she tell you *there*, along with all the other relatives—"

"*In front* of all the other relatives." Trish added her stabbing chopsticks to the firing squad at Jenn, although her air stabbing flung a chow mein noodle onto Jenn's plate.

"—rather than telling you privately beforehand?" Venus bit the head off the shrimp.

Lex spooned some black bean sauce shrimp onto a mound of rice. "Jenn, you made a lot of shrimp dishes for the party."

"And the problem with that is …?" Venus gave her a *look*.

"I can take that shrimp if you—" Trish reached for Lex's plate.

Lex *whapped* her cousin's chopsticks out of the way. "I wasn't complaining."

A faint cry sounded from Jenn's living room, and Trish got up. "Elyssa's awake. Time to feed her."

"Feed her in there, please." Lex's face was already almost as green as the sautéed Chinese broccoli.

Venus rolled her eyes. "You are such a baby. It's only breast milk. It's not blood."

"It's a bodily fluid, and I don't nag you about your Mr. Monk impressions, so stop nagging me about my neuroses." Lex took a sip of green tea, and her color improved.

"Besides, she's almost off the milk by now anyway," Trish called back to them as she exited Jenn's kitchen and entered the living room. Her coos to her daughter carried to them.

"So what are you going to do?" Venus asked Jenn.

She toyed with her shrimp and portabella mushroom tart. What a waste of time it was to work on these when no one but they were enjoying them.

Except after the way her family had treated her, she didn't *want* any of them enjoying them. So this wasn't a waste—it was actually preventing this from going to waste on ungrateful, pushy, unsympathetic …

"I want to show them that if I don't matter to them, then they don't matter to me."

"Huh?" Lex's chopstick stopped halfway to her open mouth.

"Back up, Jenn," Venus said.

Jenn set down her mushroom tart. "They wouldn't listen to me about Brad. In fact, they didn't even care. *I* didn't matter to them."

Venus looked down at her plate and chewed her lip but didn't say anything.

Because Jenn was right. "Mimi and her wonderful new boyfriend—who's a Yip, by the way, and we all know they can do no wrong—were the only ones they cared about. Not Jenn and her culinary degree—oh, except when it came to expecting me to work for Aunty Aikiko."

"But didn't you take all those night courses so you could work for her?"

"It wasn't just for her. I wanted to learn how to be a chef. I wanted to someday own my own restaurant, not take over for her."

CHAPTER THREE

"And did you tell this lovely plan to Aunty at all?" Venus drawled.

Jenn's answer stuck in her throat. "Uh, no. But in my defense, she never mentioned about me taking over the restaurant until today."

"Oh come on." Lex set down her chopsticks, loaded with a mound of noodles. "You knew that's what Aunty was expecting."

Jenn rubbed her forehead with her hand. "Yes, I know, I know. Maybe I was in denial."

"Well, what about now? What are you going to do now?" Venus speared a shrimp tempura. "If you tell me you're going to meekly quit your job to go work for Aunty, I will take this plate of shrimp and leave."

"Not without giving me some." Lex snatched one from the plate.

"Honestly, is food the only thing you guys can think about?" Trish demanded as she entered the kitchen, baby Elyssa in her arms. "This is serious. The family has majorly dissed Jenn."

Silence fell over the four of them as they watched the food grow cold.

"Not that food isn't important." Trish snatched a bacon-rolled shrimp.

They munched in silence for a while, then suddenly Trish said, "I've got it. Cater my wedding."

Jenn frowned at her. "I thought I *was* catering your wedding."

"I mean, as my *caterer.*"

Jenn blinked at her.

"She means, start your own catering business," Venus said, her eyes bright. "Trish's wedding will be your trial run."

"Use that culinary degree for your own business, not Aunty Aikiko's," Lex said.

"You don't matter to them? Well then, Aunty's restaurant doesn't matter to you," Trish added. "But who matters to you? Me! I'm your girl." She held out her fist and Jenn weakly bumped it with hers.

Not work for Aunty Aikiko? Jenn felt a weird combination of elation and terror. "But … my job." Programming paid well in the Bay Area. Catering … not so much.

"When were you going to start work at the restaurant?" Venus asked.

"Never," Jenn shot back.

"I mean before they hacked you off, genius."

"Oh. I dunno ... a month or two."

"So you were going to give notice at your computer programming job in a month or two?"

"Oh. Well, yeah." But it had been a nebulous thing in her mind. She still had a hard time believing she'd gotten her culinary degree at last.

"So what's stopping you from quitting early and starting your own catering business?"

"Health insurance." The words fell from her lips like the first cold drops of rain from a storm front.

There was a beat of thoughtful silence around the kitchen table. Snatches of memory went through her mind—driving her mom to the hospital for chemo, holding her head as she threw up into the toilet, watching her weakly sipping tea, praying for Jesus to please take the cancer away. And He had.

If Jenn worked for Aunty Aikiko, she'd have the health insurance offered to all restaurant employees. If she started her own business, she'd have to pay for her own insurance.

"Quitting my job seems irresponsible," Jenn said. "What if Mom's cancer comes back?"

"You can't live life based on 'what ifs,'" Venus said quietly. "Sometimes you just have to take a leap and go for it. If Aunty's cancer comes back, then you reevaluate and figure out your options."

"But that's ... that's scary." Jenn hated how small her voice was, but she couldn't imagine doing what Venus was suggesting. Sure, Venus was smart and driven. Trish was fearless and adventurous. Lex was gutsy and stubborn. She was ... just Jenn.

"You can't live your life being afraid, Jenn." Lex's eyes were steady. "Otherwise, you might as well bow your head like a good little Asian girl and go work for Aunty Aikiko at the restaurant. *For the rest of your life.*"

CHAPTER THREE

The words were hollow like a death sentence. Jenn shuddered. No, she couldn't do that. She wouldn't.

She turned to Venus. "Okay, Miss CEO, what do I do first?"

"You've lived your entire life in California, and you've never driven with the top down?"

The rush of the wind whipping past Jenn's RAV4 made Trish shout to be heard. In lieu of a retractable top, they'd opened the windows and the sunroof.

"I never had a convertible, doofus." Jenn navigated the winding country road at a nice, safe speed.

"We should have rented one for today." Trish tipped her head back and smiled at the sunlight dappling through the trees lining the road. "Days like these were made for convertibles."

"Since when did you drive a convertible?"

"I rode in an ex-boyfriend's Cabriolet."

Jenn giggled. "Very sexy. Which ex was this?"

"Ted. It gets even better—it was his *mother's* Cabriolet."

"Ted? I don't remember a Ted."

"You and Venus were both getting your master's degrees at Stanford at the time. And Ted had a drinking problem, so he only lasted a few weeks."

Jenn and Venus had been ecstatic to be accepted for transfer to Stanford in their junior years at San Jose State. They had taken the five-year engineering program to get their master's degrees with only one extra year of schooling as opposed to two. Venus had also gotten into the MBA program and continued with that while Jenn had immediately gotten a computer programming job. In the meantime, Trish and Lex had graduated from San Jose State and gotten jobs in their fields.

A new song came on the radio, and Trish immediately reached a hand out to turn up the volume. "I love this song."

It was "Let It Rise" by Big Daddy Weave, and the music filled the car. Trish's head fell back, her eyes closed, she flung her hands out—nearly poking Jenn's eye out—and she belted out the lyrics. It was as if her entire body was lifted in worship to God.

The sight made Jenn a little uncomfortable. Trish's complete … abandon. It made Jenn wonder a little about their faiths.

Jenn had become a Christian when she was living with Trish, Venus, and Lex during their years going to San Jose State University. Trish had come home one day, wildly excited about something she said had changed her entire life. Lex and Venus had been skeptical, but Jenn, who'd always been closer to Trish, could see that this was a *real* change, and something about the way Trish talked about it made Jenn want to know more. The four of them had gone to church that Sunday—Venus cynically said Trish only wanted to go to meet some cute guys—but they'd all come out of that service feeling different. And they'd gone back week after week, until one service there was a call for people to sign up for baptism, and all four of them had signed up.

Trish had backslidden a little a couple of years ago, but she'd renewed her relationship with Jesus since then. She was more confident, more … filled. And at times like these, watching her express her faith made Jenn feel a little *stale*.

That was silly. Jenn read her Bible every day, she went to a weekly Bible study, she went to church a lot more consistently than any of her cousins, and she knew Jesus loved her and had died for her on the cross. What else was there in being a Christian?

After the song ended, silence descended on the two of them for a time, until Jenn broke it. "It's nice not going in to work on a day like this," she admitted. "You're sure you can take off work?"

"I've accumulated too much vacation. My boss said I had to use it or lose it. And it's not like we can take a long honeymoon because of Elyssa. So I've been taking off days here and there to plan for the wedding."

"The winery knows to expect us, right?"

"Yes." Trish didn't open her eyes. "I was standing right next to Kathi when she phoned her cousin to ask if we could visit today."

Jenn privately thought Trish just wanted to get Jenn out of her house as opposed to *needing* to visit this Saratoga winery to sample their wines, even if her coworker's cousin's family owned it. They could have simply bought a bottle and tried it one night at home.

But Jenn's mom had been moaning and whining about Jenn quitting her job (last day was yesterday!), and after escaping the house like a convict, she realized it was very relaxing to go somewhere new during the day. She felt like she was playing hooky.

"How did The Conversation with Aunty Aikiko go?" Trish asked.

"Kind of frightening, actually."

"Let me guess." Trish gave her a sidelong look. "Lots of crying and wailing about you failing in your familial duty, disappointing Aunty's expectations of you working for her, being a bad niece?"

"No. None of that."

"None?" Trish turned to look at her, surprise in her face.

"That's what was frightening about it."

"You know that's not the end of it."

"Of course that's not the end of it. I'm waiting for the other shoe to drop." Despite her casual words, a thick cesspool of dread swirled in Jenn's stomach at the thought of what Aunty Aikiko would do now that she'd lost her future restaurant manager.

"You could go a little faster." Trish eyed the speedometer significantly.

"Says the woman who drives on sidewalks."

"It was only one time! And I got distracted by a false labor contraction, thank you very much, and I was only *just* easing into the intersection after the light had turned green." Trish added, "And I didn't hit anybody!"

"Well, I don't want to hit anyone either."

"There's no one to hit." Trish flung her hand out of the car at the open country fields on either side of them to push her point.

"There's the biker behind us." He was pretty far away, but Jenn could already hear the rumble of his Harley-Davidson. She glanced again in the rearview mirror and caught a twinkle of chrome.

Trish turned her passenger side mirror to get a look at him. "Now that's a nice way to ride these windy roads."

"Hey, you messed up my mirror. Put it back."

"I will when I'm done."

"You're getting married."

"Get your head out of the gutter. I'm not looking at the rider. I'm eyeing the *bike*."

He came up behind them, a relaxed figure in black leather with metal trim on his fitted jacket. The roar of the motor filled the car through the open windows.

The lane ahead of her was long and empty, so she eased to the right-ish side of the road to signal that he could pass her if he wanted.

He wanted. The motor growled, although he didn't zip past her as she expected him to. He was driving a bit cautiously for a biker, to be honest.

He passed to her left, and Jenn turned to look at him. He looked at her at the same moment.

He had the dreamiest eyes. Something about them—about the look he gave her—made her chest tighten and her breath come in faster gasps.

He didn't look away. Neither did she.

A small part of her brain squealed at her to smile, to give him any kind of encouragement. But she couldn't seem to move her facial muscles. And her jaw was in her lap, completing her dorky look.

A bumping noise … Oops, she had drifted too far to the right, and one side of the car was treading through the gravel at the side of the road.

"Jenn!"

CHAPTER THREE

She snapped her eyes forward and righted the car slowly, lest she ram into the biker to her left. Lovely way to pick up a man—run him over with her SUV. The biker passed them and moved back into the right lane.

"And you talk about me driving on sidewalks?" Trish said.

"You will have to excuse me for being distracted by the view," Jenn said loftily.

"The bike? This from the woman too terrified to even sit behind our cousin on his motorcycle?"

"It was Larry, and only an idiot wouldn't fear for her life. I meant the rider. He was gorgeous."

"You couldn't even see his face."

"Yes, I could. He had a clear-ish visor. He had beautiful eyes."

Trish groaned. "You mean the kind of eyes women would die for but men get instead? I don't want to hear about it."

"No, they were very masculine. He was dishy."

"According to the two square inches you could see of his face."

"It was love at first sight, I tell you." Jenn grinned.

"The first time I saw Spenser, I thought he was cute," Trish admitted. "But he got annoying real fast. Men do that, you know."

"I hate to tell you this, but you're marrying him."

"I didn't say the annoying was *bad*—"

Bam!

"What was that?" Trish shrieked.

"Relax, it's just a tire. We got a flat." Jenn's calm voice belied her pounding heart. She had to fight the steering wheel a bit to get the car to the side of the road.

"This lane is awful narrow," Trish said as they got out of the car. "And we're not far from a bend in the road. I hope no one comes by soon."

"Well, then, help me change this tire quickly."

Her words were drowned out by the sound of a very loud motor.

The next thing she knew, the Harley rider had pulled up beside her. She hadn't even seen him turn around to head back to them. Had he heard their tire blow out? His bike was a monstrous presence, his eyes even more intense behind his visor. He cut the engine and took off his helmet. "Need help?"

Jenn would have answered him, but her heart had stopped. And her mouth had stopped working. And she couldn't blink, either. And her lungs might have collapsed, too, because she was getting dizzy from lack of oxygen.

He was *über*-dishy.

Chestnut hair. Dark, dreamy eyes. A firm jaw framing a mobile mouth with fine laugh lines at the corners.

His gaze caught hers like a hand cupping her face. He didn't look away. Neither did she.

Suddenly a kick to her calf—*à la* Trish—made Jenn blink. "Oh." He had asked a question. What had it been? "Uh, yes. We need help. If you have time."

"I don't mind." His voice had a light tone, as if he made quippy jokes often or poked fun at himself a lot. "You're right near where the road curves, so it's a bit dangerous. Better to get a spare tire on quickly."

He had a fascinating little divot in his chin …

Trish delivered another not-so-subtle kick to Jenn's ankle. "Er … thanks. I really appreciate the help."

He smiled then, and Jenn was completely lost. His laugh lines were deep, framing his bright, slightly shy smile. She suddenly felt an overwhelming urge to grab his face and kiss him.

Oh my goodness, she had to get a hold of herself. Her neck started to burn.

"So where are you two headed today?" he asked as he fiddled with the locking mechanism to unhitch her spare tire from the back of the SUV.

"We're going to Armstrong Winery," Trish said brightly. "I'm tasting wines to see if I want to order them for my wedding, and Jenn's my caterer."

He glanced not at Trish but at Jenn. "You should go to the Castillo Winery just down the road. It's my uncle's."

"Your uncle owns Castillo?" Jenn perked up. "I've seen his wines but never tasted one." She seemed to recall that one of his Pinot Noir blends won an award last year.

He winked at her. "It's better than Armstrong."

Jenn laughed. "Of course you'd say that."

"I'm completely unbiased." Suddenly he frowned down at the spare, which he'd dropped on the ground from the hitch. "Your spare is flat."

"What?" Jenn bent and pressed against the tire. It gave like a marshmallow. "But it's new. I got five new tires only a few months ago."

"I'm afraid you'll have to tow your car. Have you got AAA?"

"I guess we'll miss our tasting appointment." Trish pulled out her phone. "Oh, no. My battery's dead."

"You can use mine," Jenn said.

"No, I have the winery's number on my phone. You don't have it, do you?"

Jenn shook her head, then turned back to the handsome stranger. "You don't happen to have your competitor's phone number, do you?"

He smiled again, and Jenn's stomach flipped. "I'll do you one better. I'll ask my cousin to come pick you up and take you to the winery."

"We can't ask you to do that," Trish protested. "You—or rather, your cousin—would have to wait for us and then take us back to the car."

"I don't mind. It's my day off today. I'm also good friends with Barry Armstrong, and I can make sure he treats you right, as opposed to their normal tasting room manager. And then you'll come to Castillo to taste our wines, right?"

Trish laughed. "Okay!"

Jenn wanted to match her exuberance, but she worried about inconveniencing this man and his cousin. She always felt like a wet blanket around Trish. And she didn't even know the guy's name.

She waited until he had called his cousin and disconnected his cell phone. "I'm Jennifer Lim," she said, extending a hand.

"Edward Castillo."

His clasp was warm—no, hot. But not sweaty hot or uncomfortable hot. More like energizingly hot. His palm was slightly rough, as if he spent a lot of time doing rough jobs, maybe working in the vineyard. And he seemed reluctant to let go of her hand, which gave her heart a little blip of *Whoopee!*

"I'm Trish Sakai. Jenn and I are cousins."

A slow smile seemed aimed at Jenn. "I could tell."

Really? Trish was ten times prettier—most people said so. The best they could ever say about Jenn was that she had a deep, husky Lauren Bacall voice. Somehow Edward's words seemed like a compliment she might actually believe about herself.

His cousin, David, arrived within only a few minutes. "That was fast," Jenn remarked as a pickup truck rattled to a halt in front of them.

"The back entrance to Castillo is only a mile up the road," Edward said. "Armstrong is about ten miles beyond that."

Trish was about to hop into the truck, but then she turned and gave Jenn that coy, *I'm going to do something you'll hate but it'll be good for you* look. "Jenn, didn't you tell me you've always wanted to ride a Harley?"

What?! A pulse of abject fear swallowed her exclamation.

Trish turned guileless eyes to Edward. "I didn't mean to put you on the spot, but if you'd be willing to indulge a girl …"

He jumped on the suggestion. "I'd be happy to." He extended a hand to Jenn. "I have an extra helmet with me, too."

That hand was a tempter, enticing her onto that chrome-gilded death trap on two very small wheels. But the hand was confident, and its owner even more so. And while the death trap would have normally sent her screaming in the opposite direction, that hand pulled her like a truffle to a chocoholic.

"S-sure." She gave him her hand, which felt numb and cold.

He squeezed her fingers slightly—she wasn't sure what that meant. Her brain was firing *Run away! Run away!* synapses like exploding fireworks, but she followed him to the bike.

CHAPTER THREE

He slid a helmet over her head, its weight making her neck feel fragile and breakable, especially on a doorless machine going at thirty miles an hour …

No, she couldn't think about that. She'd be with Edward, who seemed like a safe … well, she didn't know if he was a safe driver. He seemed like a safe … no, she wasn't quite sure he was a safe person either, which she had to admit added to his appeal.

Um … God, keep us safe!

She climbed on board.

CHAPTER FOUR

S HE TOOK HIS breath away. In more ways than one.

Or maybe it was because Edward had sucked in his gut the entire short ride to Armstrong Winery, because she'd been clenching him around his middle so tightly. She hadn't seemed the flirty type. Actually, he would have interpreted her touch as a death grip if she hadn't said she'd always wanted to ride a Harley.

She'd socked him in the stomach with her first glance at him, when he'd been passing her truck and she'd caught his eye. Something about her made him think of the moon over the vineyards on a clear night in summer. She gave him that same sense of peace and rightness and belonging.

He'd never felt this way about a woman before. It exhilarated him. It scared the rips off his jeans.

They pulled into the long driveway to the tasting rooms of Armstrong, but he led David to the back of the property to one of the main office buildings instead. The noise of the Harley brought Barry out of his office into the parking lot. "Oh my garlic," he exclaimed. "Look at you."

CHAPTER FOUR

Here was a good excuse to show off his birthday present to Barry. Edward parked the bike and made to get off, but Jennifer's arms were still in a vise lock around his midsection. He paused. "Uh …"

Jennifer started. "Oh. Sorry." She slipped away from him, and the day got cooler.

"When did you get this bike?" Barry demanded with a wide, envious smile.

"Today. Late birthday present from Uncle Ron."

"Lucky dog." Barry bent to take a closer look at the engine.

"Happy belated birthday," Jennifer said softly. She had a deep, sultry voice that made him think of old black and white movies.

"Thanks." His coolness factor had skyrocketed just because of the bike and leather. Except how would she react if she knew he was normally not a mysterious biker dude but just a rather nerdy farmer?

David had parked the truck, and Trish climbed out. "Barry, this is Trish Sakai and her cousin, Jennifer Lim."

"Call me Jenn," she said, taking his hand.

Jenn. That sounded more like her than Jennifer.

"We have an appointment with your tasting room manager," Trish said.

"They *had* an appointment with your tasting room manager," Edward said. "I told them you'd treat them better, Barry."

Barry's eyes narrowed as he surveyed first the women, then Edward. "Why aren't they at your winery?"

He snatched at the opportunity. "Oh, so you don't want them here? No prob—"

"I didn't say that, chump," Barry replied with a playful chop to his arm.

"Actually, Edward and David are helping us out after our car broke down a few miles down the road," Jenn said.

He chose to think of it as an act of God that their car got a flat only seconds after he'd passed them on the road. He'd been reluctant

31

to continue on his way after that first startling look he exchanged with Jenn, but he didn't really relish being flattened by an oncoming car.

And now he had the next hour with them at Armstrong and hopefully another hour at Castillo. He'd never before felt this kind of urgency to get to know a girl—then again, he'd never before been flattened by a first look from a woman, either.

They all trooped to the tasting room, where Barry served them himself. He also opened a few bottles of reserve wines normally not available for tasting, giving Edward and David an arch look as if to challenge them to be more gracious a host than he was being.

Edward and David ribbed Barry all during the girls' wine tasting, but Barry gave back as good as he got.

"Hey Barry, your Pinot Grigio tastes less like lemonade today."

"Last time, I did give you lemonade."

"Barry, the Zinfandel has finally learned not to bite."

"The zin learned its manners. I can't say as much about Castillo's Cabernet Sauvignon."

When they were tasting a rather nice pinot noir, Jenn nodded. "That would taste good with a nice, sharp cheese. Maybe a goat cheese."

"One of the Castillo pinot noirs pairs well with our farm's goat cheese," Edward interjected before Barry could say anything.

"You make cheese?"

"We have both cows and goats, and we make artisan cheeses for our wine and cheese pairing menu."

Jenn's eyes lit up like amber jewels. "Wine and cheese pairing?"

Trish turned to Edward. "Maybe we can do that when we come to Castillo Winery after this."

If he hadn't been listening to Trish talking about her wedding plans, he'd have thought she was flirting with him. But the quick look she gave Jenn, then moving back to Edward, answered his questions.

Bride-to-be was playing matchmaker with the caterer and the winemaker. Sounded like a nursery rhyme. Except he liked the sound of that—caterer and winemaker.

Barry cut in with a "You're better off drinking drain cleaner than Castillo's wines," but David replied with "They're saving the best for last."

"Let's go," Edward said. "Unless you'd like to try more of Barry's poison."

Barry responded with a hand clutching his heart. "You're killing me, Edward."

Maybe at Castillo's he'd be able to chat with Jenn …

Suddenly two cell phones went off, both with song ringtones. He actually knew them both from listening to the Christian radio station—Trish's phone played "Fool for You" by Nichole Nordeman, and Jenn's played "Not Gonna Let You Down" by Building 429.

She was a Christian? They were both Christians?

The heavens opened up with an angelic chorus singing something loud and magnificent and probably in Latin. Because Jenn was a Christian. Edward started to wonder if God Himself had blown her tire just for him.

"Oh no!" both cousins said in unison into their phones.

His shoulders felt like a couple fertilizer bags had fallen on them.

The two women looked at each other with identical expressions of dismay. In that moment, they looked like twins.

Trish disconnected first. "Elyssa fell down my parents' stairs!"

"Is she okay?" Jenn asked, her eyes wide.

"Mom took her to the hospital. We have to go meet them."

Jenn nodded, but her eyes were distracted even as she shoved her phone back in her pocket.

"Who was that?" Trish asked her.

"Mom." Jenn had turned white, but her eyes burned with a strange fire. "My one goat … has turned into *three*."

The good thing about being a cousin was that Jenn had lots of blackmail options in her arsenal.

She'd already called Larry twelve times and left messages on his cell phone, so she resorted to e-mail. But not just ineffectual demands for him to call her about the goat. No, the fact he wasn't taking her calls required more lethal shots. Luckily, Larry being still in college and living in the dorms presented extra fodder for her devious mind.

She sat at her computer, flipping through digital photos, until she found a few particularly juicy ones, namely the ones involving the extended family's trip to Hawaii. Larry was showing off for some bikini-clad babes, unaware that the swim trunks he'd borrowed from a cousin had a huge rip in them. She attached them to an e-mail and typed in the subject line:

I will send these to your dorm mates if you don't call me

After she sent it, she cocked her head and regarded her sent folder. Making threats wasn't anything special coming from, say, Lex or Venus, but she knew she lacked a certain amount of fear factor in her cousin's eyes.

She sent another e-mail:

I mean it!!!! Call me!!!!

She knew he was on his computer because she got onto Facebook and saw he was online and "available to chat." However, mere seconds after she had signed into Facebook, he signed off of chat.

Coward.

Ten minutes. He was deliberately ignoring her. Even the picture of him with the Polwarth sheep hadn't been enough to force him to call her.

Jenn glowered at her laptop screen, then stood and paced her bedroom, avoiding the pile of cookbooks on the floor and also the box containing new baking pans she'd bought to make Trish's wedding cake.

She didn't really want to send the pictures to Larry's dorm mates. Which Larry probably knew. If Venus had sent the e-mail, Larry would have been dialing before the last picture even downloaded. Maybe Jenn should have asked Venus …

No, this was her problem. She had to stop relying on her cousins all the time to help her and be her "muscle." She needed to develop some "muscle" too.

Fine. He'd called her bluff. She'd up the ante.

She called his mother, Aunt Glenda.

"Hi, Aunt Glenda!"

"Oh, hello, Jenn." A little guarded in her tone. Was Jenn really surprised? The news that Jenn wasn't going to work at the restaurant had probably reached Aunt Glenda within seconds of Jenn getting off the phone with Aunty Aikiko last week.

Jenn put on her brightest *I'm such a properly obedient Asian niece that I'll scrub your bathroom floor with a toothbrush* voice. "Aunty, I'm going to San Jose State this afternoon, and I know how much you hate driving in downtown San Jose, so I wondered if there was anything you wanted me to take to Larry at his dorm?"

It earned her a grudging "That's very nice of you, Jenn. In fact, I do have a load of laundry Larry needs right away."

"Great! I'll come by and pick it up in a few minutes. Is there anything else?" She gave a thoughtful pause. "Any special momento Larry might have forgotten in his room that he might need?"

Aunty always treated Larry, her only son, as if he still couldn't feed himself with a fork if she weren't there to help him. Now, Jenn counted on it. "Is there any kind of memento Larry might need for exams next week?"

"There are exams next week?"

"My cousin Mimi said they were soon." If "soon" meant six weeks away.

"Oh, he always gets so stressed when there are exams. Last time, he bought so many pizzas for all-nighters that he needed to borrow money."

Pizzas, huh? More like drinkable sustenance. "Is there anything I could bring him to help him?"

"Oh, I have the perfect thing. When he was in high school, he'd lie on his yellow pony rug in the living room to study."

"Wonderful." Even Jenn hadn't known about the yellow pony rug, although Larry had let slip once that he had a lucky charm for when he had to study for finals in his senior year. "Aunty, why don't you call him and let him know I'll be by this afternoon with his laundry and the yellow pony rug."

"I'll do that right now. Thanks, Jenn."

Jenn hung up her cell phone and counted the seconds. Fifteen seconds for Aunty to ask how he was doing, another twenty seconds while she rambled on and Larry tried to get her off the phone, then ten seconds when Aunty remembered why she'd called her darling boy and told him about the laundry. And the yellow pony rug. Five seconds for Larry to realize what Jenn had done and give some excuse for needing to get off the phone right away—maybe a fire drill or an e-mail from his professor.

Her phone rang. Caller ID: Larry.

"I was thinking of draping the rug across the couch in your dorm's common room," Jenn said. "Maybe with a note pinned to it saying, 'This is Larry's study partner.'"

"Jenn," he said with false heartiness, "you're not like that. You wouldn't do that to me, would you?" She could almost hear the sweat dripping down his face.

"Of course I would. I would consider it ample repayment for the *goats in my backyard*."

"Aw, but Pookie's awful cute, isn't he?"

"Pookie is a she, and she tripled yesterday."

"Tripled? Uh … congratulations?"

He was a little too unsurprised by that. "Did Brad know she was pregnant?"

"No, of course not."

"You are going to call him and tell him to come get his goat today."

"Today? That's too short notice—"

"Today or else the little yellow pony is going to be galloping through the front door of your dorm."

He gave a painful groan into the phone.

Mom's soft knock on her bedroom door.

Jenn stood up but finished her conversation with her cousin before opening it. "I mean it, Larry! That goat is eating me out of house and home. If Brad doesn't get it from me today, it's going to the Humane Society, and his mother will blow like an aerosol can in a microwave. And you know what? I don't care if they are Yips. I'm not keeping their goat another day." She disconnected the phone just as she opened her bedroom door.

Aunty Aikiko stood next to her mom.

Jenn's jaw clenched. Well, what did she expect? On the phone, Aunty had *said* "You should do whatever is best for you, Jenn." But what she *meant* was "I'll let this go for now and then snipe in with a new argument later to break down your defenses (you puny human)."

Jenn tried to smile, but it felt like her face cracked in half. "Hi, Aunty."

"Jenn, I'm so glad I caught you at home. I have a favor to ask."

Jenn felt like she was waiting for a soufflé to collapse. "Why don't we go out into the living room?" Jenn made to move past her, but Aunty stood her ground.

"No, why don't I speak to you privately in your room?"

No way would she be secluded with Aunty in her bedroom. That was like inviting a tiger to sit down for a comfortable chat in a confined space.

Besides, this was *her* house. She'd paid the majority of the mortgage payments since Dad was gone, and she could dictate who she entertained where.

"Aunty, I was just on my way out. Let's talk in the living room." Jenn forcibly thrust herself between Aunty and Mom and led the way to the living room, leaving them no choice but to follow.

They sat. Maybe Jenn should have likened Aunty to a spider rather than a tiger. She looked at Jenn as if she were a fly. "What did you need?" Not *What can I do for you?* She hoped Aunty got the hint, but probably not.

"We haven't had a vacation in years, and we'd like to take the boys to Disneyland."

Jenn cleared her throat. "Aren't they a little old for Disneyland?"

"Ryden is sixteen," Aunty said blithely of her youngest.

"Er … and so Daniel, Jared, Rick, and Ryden all want to go to Disneyland?"

"Oh, yes, they've been cooped up at the house for too long."

Actually, Daniel traveled extensively for his engineering job and was only living at home because of his recent divorce. Jared had gotten laid off, so he'd been out to employment agencies and interviews for the past several months, and Rick was a senior at the University of California at Berkeley and was only home every third weekend. Jenn had to breathe through her nose slowly and carefully before she could unclench her teeth. "What about Mimi?"

"Oh, she doesn't need to go."

The wording made Jenn frown. Aunty was always that way with Mimi. Was it any wonder the girl had become a little wild? At least she and Lex had been roommates for a couple years, but that had ended a year ago when Lex eloped with Aiden.

"So what was the favor you wanted to ask?" Jenn already knew, even before Aunty jumped at the question.

"We want you to take over the restaurant while we go on vacation."

"No, sorry." The words shot out before she even finished the request.

"Jenn!" Mom objected.

Aunty's mouth had frozen open.

"No, I'm too busy setting up my catering business." Jenn knew the "vacation" was just a flimsy excuse to get her working at the restaurant. When they came back from "Disneyland," Aunty would come up with other excuses why they couldn't come back to work, and Jenn would be forced to either stay there or leave the restaurant high and dry.

Aunty's face turned a dark red like an *azuki* bean. Mom sighed and shook her head, probably wondering what alien had abducted her daughter and left this foreign surrogate in her place.

A reckless streak prompted Jenn to add, "You should ask Mimi to take over."

"Mimi wouldn't know the first thing what to do," Aunty snapped.

"Actually, considering Mimi works there more often than all her brothers combined, I think she'd know exactly what to do."

"She couldn't possibly run the restaurant alone—"

"I'm almost positive Jared would be happy to forego Disneyland to help her."

Aunty gave her a wrathful look.

Jenn met it with a guileless expression. She stood up. "Sorry to run off, Aunty, but I have some errands. Good-bye!"

As she picked up her purse and exited the house, she burst out the front door like Daniel escaping the lion's den. God had helped her be brave and stand firm. She'd never fall prey to her relatives' manipulations again.

CHAPTER FIVE

THE GOATS WERE still there.

Jenn mutinously shoveled goat feed into the feeding trough (which, to the goat, looked mysteriously like an old bucket).

One of the two babies, skittish before, suddenly came up to her, hopping in a circle around her, leaping and twisting in midair. One of his acrobatics nudged her in the back of the leg, making her sway on her feet. She glared down at the tiny creature.

He seemed to be smiling at her in a mysterious goat way. Really, he was quite cute. She patted him on the head, which he endured with a condescending grace for all of half a second before bounding off to play with his sibling.

Well, she'd given Larry the day, and he had failed her. He had to face the consequences, dire though they may be. Jenn realized she was actually looking forward to this.

She hopped in her car, the ratty, fluffy yellow pony rug draped over her backseat. Ah, the sight of it filled her with such malicious joy.

On the drive to downtown San Jose, however, her phone rang. She didn't want to take her attention off the road to rummage in her purse and look at the caller ID on her cell phone, so she just hit the answer button on her Bluetooth. "Hello?"

"Hi, Jenn, it's Aunty Yoshiko. Bethany has a cooking project she needs to do next week, and we wondered if you'd be able to help her?"

"No."

A beat of silence. "Er ... what did you say?"

"No, sorry, Aunty. I'm too busy." Besides which, the last time she'd "helped" Bethany with a project, she'd ended up doing half of it because the lazy brat's sloppy efforts would have ruined not only her project but also Jenn's springform pan, which she'd let her borrow since she didn't have one.

"But ..." Aunty sputtered incoherently. "But Bethany needs you."

As if that was reason enough for Jenn to drop everything? "I'm too busy, Aunty. You'll have to help her yourself"—and get those two-inch-long acrylic nails dirty, imagine that?—"or ask someone else."

"There's no one else to ask."

"I'm sure there is. I have fifty-seven cousins on the Sakai side."

Aunty gave a gasp of indignation.

"Bye, Aunty!" Jenn hit the Bluetooth button to disconnect the call.

That felt wonderful! Jenn neatly changed lanes to pass a slow car.

Another phone call. "Hello?"

"Hi, Jenn, this is Mrs. Hoshiwara from church. I'm gathering names for the church bake sale to raise money for Vacation Bible School. Can you help us out again this year?"

It was on the tip of her tongue to say yes. After all, Mrs. Hoshiwara had been nothing but nice to her since Jenn started going to church.

But wasn't this all about the Liberation of Jenn? No longer slave to the needs of others? She'd just denied two aunties—two blood relations. Surely the church would understand?

"I'm sorry, Mrs. Hoshiwara, but I'm afraid I'm too busy. I just quit my job, and I'm starting a catering business."

"Oh, how wonderful!"

Her enthusiastic approval made Jenn's stomach gurgle uncomfortably.

"I'm so glad you're doing this, Jenn," she continued. "You're so talented in the kitchen."

"Thanks, Mrs. Hoshiwara."

"Of course you wouldn't have time to make something for the bake sale."

Actually, she probably could whip up a batch of cookies pretty darn quick … No, she was being liberated. She had to stick to her guns.

So why did it feel so different to tell Mrs. Hoshiwara no? It hadn't felt like this with either of her aunties.

"Well, I'll see you at church on Sunday," Mrs. Hoshiwara said.

"Uh … yeah." Jenn actually hadn't been to church in a couple of weeks because she'd stayed up late doing things—Trish's wedding, her business license, applying for a small business loan …

"Bye, Jenn!" She hung up.

Jenn could make it up to her next year, make a couple cakes or something. Right?

Speaking of cakes, she needed to start her trial runs of Trish's wedding cake to make sure she could get everything done right the day before the wedding. Plus she was eager to try out those new cake pans.

Parking in downtown was almost impossible—what a surprise—so she had to park several blocks away and hoof it to Larry's dorm with his ginormous laundry bag and the stinkin' yellow pony rug trailing behind her. When she entered his dormitory front entrance, she was surprised to find not only Larry but also Brad waiting to pounce on her.

And not just Brad, but a couple quarterback-sized Yip cousins, too.

The rug was ripped from her hands, but unfortunately no one grabbed the laundry bag. So she dumped it on the ground and kicked it aside.

She addressed the slimy fink ratworm Brad. "So you could drop off the goat at my house, and you can drive into downtown San Jose, but you can't come pick up your animal?"

Brad just laughed and flashed that *I'm better than you because my daddy makes enough in a day to buy your house* look. "Jenn, your bitterness over losing me has really pervaded your life."

She had a strange, fierce buzzing in her ears, and her voice came from a long way away. "Losing you? More like good riddance."

"Thanks so much for bringing that for me, Jenn," Larry said in a triumphantly smarmy voice. "Now I can burn it without needing to sneak it out of the house first."

"If you hadn't had the linebackers over there, you'd have had to fight me for it. And I'd win."

Larry only smirked. "I needed the protection because you've obviously gone over the edge. You're crazy and dangerous. Who knows what you'd do?"

She did feel dangerous. Worse, she felt more than a little crazy. "Brad, you can pick up your goat at the Humane Society." She turned to leave.

"Oh no, you won't."

"Stop me," she flung over her shoulder.

"Your grandmother will."

She froze in her tracks. The linebackers snickered.

Turning to face him, she pinned him with a glare that should have seared him like crème brûlée. "Explain yourself."

"Your Aunt Aikiko called my mother and said you had told your Grandma Sakai that you were ... what were the words she used? Oh yes, 'thrilled' to keep Great-Aunt Chin's goat. So when Larry called me and I called Mom, she was understandably confused about the threats to take it to the Humane Society."

Jenn's mind raced. Aunty Aikiko must have overheard her talking to Larry on her phone and drawn her own conclusions. Aunty wasn't close friends with Brad's mother, but she'd managed to get her to take her call anyway.

Jenn had to admit it was extremely clever. In invoking Grandma's name to Brad's mom, Jenn couldn't get rid of the goat, or else she'd risk

Mrs. Yip talking to Grandma about Jenn. It would put Grandma in a very awkward position, despite the fact that she probably didn't even know about this goat feud.

Her head was on fire. Her hair was burning. She really did expect laser beams to shoot out of her eyes as she glared at first Brad then Larry. She turned and moved toward the door slowly, keeping an iron hold on her raging desire to run around in a circle shrieking her frustration.

Just before she left, Larry called out, "Hey, you forgot your bag." He kicked the bag of laundry she'd dropped.

He didn't even realize it was his bag of laundry, the doofus-brain. She was about to snarl at him what he could do with it, but then an idea of such brilliance struck her, she wondered where that brilliance had been when she was trying to pass her physics classes.

She met Larry with a tight face, praying she didn't betray her elation. "Oh, sorry. You don't want that there, do you?"

He snorted. "No, get it out of here."

"I'll get that out of your way." She slung the bag over her shoulder and walked out of the dorm.

She had to walk several blocks off campus to one of the fraternity houses. A nice-looking kid sat on the front steps, studying.

Jenn paused. He looked a little too respectable, but the bag was too heavy for her to try to find another frat house. "Hi."

He looked up. "Hi. Can I help you?"

"I need a few guys with a little creativity."

"To do what?"

She held out the duffle bag. "These clothes belong to Larry, a freshman living in Building B. I need you to do something very creative and very public with them."

A slow smile spread across his face, turning him from angelic into downright devilish. "Larry, you said? Your wish is my command."

44

CHAPTER FIVE

"His tighty-whities ended up on a flagpole," Jenn told her cousins the next day over lunch. "They had written his name on them with Sharpie markers."

Lex chortled. "Think he'll tell his mom?"

"And admit his pajamas were decorated and waving outside the art building? I don't think so." Jenn passed them a plate of cheese spread and crackers. "Here, try this. I'm thinking of using this for the wedding."

Trish tried one. "Delish, but remember, Mom's on a special diet because of her heart attack."

"Oh, nuts. I forgot."

"But we'll eat this." Lex grabbed one. "Tell you what, Jenn. I'll tell one of the web guys at my workplace. He has the kind of sense of humor that'll do a good job making fun of the 'mysterious Larry's clothing' all over San Jose State campus."

Venus had a cream-laden cat expression. "He'll have to buy new underwear."

"You think?"

"Do you really believe he had another load of laundry at his dorm? No, he took everything home for his mom to wash for him."

"You don't feel just a little sorry for him?" Trish asked, although she didn't look all that sorry.

"Why should I? His own mother told him I was bringing his laundry to him, yet he told me to get rid of the bag. I told Aunty Glenda that, too."

Lex's eyes grew round. "You did?"

Jenn nodded, drizzling sauce over the steamed asparagus. "I called her when I was driving home. 'Aunty, I don't understand it, but Larry didn't want the bag of laundry. He told me to get rid of it. So I gave it to a boy sitting on the steps of a house, who said he could use the clothes.'" Jenn slid the platter onto the kitchen table. "She was a little surprised, but she told me thank you."

"Jenn, you are becoming downright devious." Lex grabbed an asparagus spear with her fingers, then dropped it on her plate. "Hot!"

"Use your fork, neanderthal," Venus told her. "So what are you going to do about the goat?"

Jenn sighed. "I don't know. Keep it, I guess."

Trish rolled her eyes. "Honestly, sometimes I wonder where your brain is. You're a cook—you have a *nursing* goat." Trish gave an *Isn't it obvious?* twirl of her fork.

All three cousins stared blankly at her.

"Oh for goodness' sake. What have the 'girls'"—Trish gestured to her chest—"been producing for the past several months?"

"Oooooh." The lightbulb blazed in Jenn's head. "How much milk does a goat produce a day? How do you milk a goat? Do I need to give her special food?"

Silence around the table.

Well, yeah, the audience wasn't exactly farmers. "How can I find out?"

Trish's eyes lit up. "Edward."

"Edward?" "Who's Edward?" Venus and Lex pounced on his name.

"What would Edward know about goats?" Jenn asked Trish, ignoring them.

"He mentioned his family makes artisan cheese, stupid. Remember?"

"Who. Is. Edward." Venus pinned Jenn and then Trish with a lethal boardroom glare that probably got all the subordinates at her company leaping to do her bidding.

Trish regaled them with what had happened two days ago in Saratoga.

"And you didn't even tell us?" Lex squealed.

"Did you at least get his digits?" Venus demanded.

"Yeah, he gave me his card."

Trish clapped her hands. "He didn't give it to me. That's wonderful!" She beamed at his neglect of her.

The stirring in her chest reminded her of the wee hours of Christmas morning, waiting for Mom and Dad to wake up so she could leave her bedroom and tear into her presents. Edward wasn't exactly a present, but she looked forward to seeing him more than getting her Easy-Bake Oven.

Maybe instead of giving Larry's clothes to a bunch of sadistic frat boys, she should have thanked him.

"Hello?"

Edward's voice made her insides feel like butter in a crepe pan. "Hi, it's Jenn. Jennifer Lim. Remember me?"

"Hey, gorgeous."

No, not mere melted butter, but a cinnamon roll hot from the oven with iced sugar glazing dripping down the sides. "H-hi."

"I was hoping you'd call."

Now she felt like a total dweeb because she had called him because she needed something from him, not because she'd had the courage to call him earlier just to chat. Or casually suggest a date. Or verify he was single. Or ask him if he wanted children. "Um … I meant to call earlier, but things have been a little crazy."

"The goats?"

The stupid reason she hadn't been able to see his winery? Yeah, those goats. "I've been trying to get rid of them, but now I can't."

"Why not?"

She sighed. "It's a long story."

"I have time."

Oh, good gracious, his voice made her want to pool on the floor.

Get a hold of yourself, Jenn. You are independent. A business owner. Confident. She turned on her best Lauren Bacall impression. "Do you want me to tell you while you teach me how to milk her?"

Somehow that seemed a lot sexier in her head.

Luckily, he laughed. "I'd be happy to. I'm working on the back vineyards today, but how about tomorrow morning?"

"Uh ... do you mind if my aunties are around?"

"Why, do they bite?"

"Noooo ... but Aunty Makiko usually says whatever's on her mind no matter who else is around to hear it, and she'll probably rip me a new one for quitting my job and not working for my aunty's restaurant."

"Whoa. That sounds almost as complicated as my brother asking two different girls to prom on top of Mama arranging for him to take one of her friend's daughters."

Jenn laughed. "Did he really?"

"Yup, so be sure to ask him when you meet him."

When, not if. The gooey feeling returned to Jenn's stomach. "We'll also be outside with the goat while my aunties will be inside helping Mom fold paper cranes for Trish's wedding."

"I'll be there." He paused. "Did you want me to arrive early? Before they get there?"

Give the man a gold star. "That would be great, if you don't mind getting here at eight?"

"See you then, Jenn."

Jenn collapsed on her bed, cradling her phone against her chest like a Bella pining for her vampire, Edward. Maybe she could invite him to lunch. Because if she really wanted to induce him to kiss her, she didn't think a good place was Pookie's udder.

CHAPTER SIX

NOT EDWARD, BUT her Aunty Makiko stood outside the front door, looking like a schoolteacher about to take sadistic pleasure in breaking a wooden ruler over some student's knuckles. Namely, Jenn's.

She whipped her hands behind her back. "Hi, Aunty. You're early."

A few feet behind them, Edward peered over their shoulders with a helpless shrug that dislodged the coil of rope he'd slung over his quite yummy shoulders. He silently mimicked a fistfight and getting socked in the jaw by the aunty wrestling to get to the door first.

Jenn tempered her giggle into a smile, but it only seemed to deepen Aunty Makiko's disfavorable glare. "Jennifer, I came early to speak to you."

The *Kill Bill* swordfight theme clicked on in her head.

The last thing she wanted was to rehash her decision not to work for Aunty Aikiko in front of Edward, because this was going to get ugly. And while she was mentally preparing for a confrontation, she shrank from airing the dirty laundry in front of a guy who might just decide her stimulating company wasn't worth her crazy, high-drama family.

"Aunty, can we talk later? My friend, Edward, is here to help me with Pookie." She gestured behind them.

Edward's eyebrows rose, and he mouthed, *Pookie?* at Jenn, but when Aunty turned around, he smiled charmingly.

Aunty Makiko gave him a long look that made his smile harden.

Jenn's teeth clenched. She was supposed to honor her elders, but when they were this rude—! He'd dressed in old jeans and a faded shirt because he'd be helping her with a goat, after all, but there was no cause to stare like he'd come stark naked.

Finally, Aunty Makiko turned—no greeting to Edward—and passed Jenn into the house.

Jenn chewed her lip and whispered, "I'm sorry."

Edward's face was grave, but he tried to smile and shrug it off. "It's not your fault."

But she had asked him to come here, it had happened on her front doorstep, and she was *related* to the woman. That was all.

"Jenn, close the door. There's a draft," Aunty Makiko yelled from the living room.

"Come in." Jenn stepped aside so Edward could enter the house. "We'll head straight into the backyard."

That was the plan, anyway. Aunty Makiko had other ideas.

Mom, bless her heart, was trying to distract her. "Makiko, here's the origami paper. Trish said her colors were pale green and peach, so I got both—"

"Not now, Yuki," she said irritably. "Jennifer, I need to talk to you."

"Mom, this is Edward Casti—"

Aunty Makiko interrupted, "You've got a lot of explaining to do."

This was like a bad sitcom. "No, I don't," she said calmly.

Mom's eyes popped out of her head while Aunty Makiko's nostrils flared. "What did you say?" she demanded in a horrible voice.

Quaking in her Crocs wasn't going to get her anywhere, so Jenn leaned on one foot and crossed her ankles to still the tremors. "I said—"

"I heard what you said, you ungrateful child."

CHAPTER SIX

Jenn tried to damp down her irritation. What was with her family? Really! "How am I ungrateful?" Not to mention being over thirty should mean her aunties would stop calling her "girl" and "child," for goodness' sake.

"After all Aunty Aikiko has done for you—"

"She didn't do anything." Jenn fought to talk through her tight jaw. "I paid for all my culinary schooling. I worked overtime to get my job done while taking classes. I put my schooling on hold while Mom went through chemo. Aunty Aikiko didn't do a thing for me."

"She offered you a job at her restaurant!"

As if that was on par with the Holy Grail. "And I refused. The problem with that is …?"

Behind Aunty Makiko's back, Mom tried to signal Jenn to shut up with a finger slicing across her neck.

"She was expecting you to work for her," Aunty Makiko said.

"She never actually asked me. She simply assumed I was going to culinary school for the sole purpose of working for her." Jenn caught Edward's embarrassed eye. "We'll be in the backyard, Mom." She grabbed Edward and hauled him out of the living room.

"I'm sorry," she said as she stomped down the back porch steps and stalked across the postage stamp backyard. "Aunty Makiko doesn't know when to keep her mouth shut."

"I have an aunt like that," he said. "Although Aunty Elena usually wants to talk about her latest gall bladder problems rather than scolding someone."

Jenn reluctantly smiled. "I'd prefer the gall bladder."

"Me too."

The goats sheltered under the apple tree (or what was left of it after eating all the low-hanging branches they could reach), where Jenn shoveled out their feed into the bucket. "Do I need to give Pookie anything extra now that she's nursing?"

Edward regarded her steadily for a long moment. "Pookie? Really?"

51

She rolled her eyes. "News flash—I didn't name her."

"True." He reached into his back pocket and handed her a folded piece of paper. "I asked Aunty Lorena to write down what she fed her nursing goats so you can find it at the feed store."

"Thanks." A man who read her mind? His one flaw was probably a tendency to fart at the dinner table or something like that.

He unslung the rope from his shoulder. "Let's tether her and see what she does."

To Jenn's eyes, it seemed Pookie threw a major tantrum, but Edward said, "Good, looks like she's been tethered before. She may have been milked, too." He upended the empty feed bucket. "Sit."

Jenn eyed the close proximity to Pookie's back leg. "You sit."

"I'm going to be at her other side to prevent her from kicking you."

"Oh." Jenn sat.

"Now grab the teat gently. Don't tug at it."

It felt leathery and foreign.

"You're going to squeeze the milk out of the teat in a smooth motion from top to bottom … No, squeeze harder. Like pushing toothpaste out of a tube."

"You're sure I'm not going to hurt—Oh!" A stream of milk shot out of the teat and bounced on the dirt ground. "I did it!" She kept staring at it. "Is that all?"

"You have to let go of the teat so more milk can flow into it."

"Oh." She let go, and it slowly thickened like a memory foam cushion getting back to its original shape. She squeezed again, and another shot of milk came out.

"Good. Now grab two of them and try to get into a rhythm with alternating teats—squeeze, release, squeeze rel—"

"You quit your job to start your own catering company?" Aunty Makiko's voice roared as if she were calling the cows to come home rather than calling just across the tiny yard.

She hadn't known that already? Mom must have let it slip, assuming it was common knowledge. Jenn didn't even deign to look at Aunty, concentrating on the two soft-ish, leathery teats in her hand. *Squeeze, release* ... "I'm calling it Jenn's Apoplexy-Inducing Brainchild."

She had to wait a few seconds for Aunty's "What?!" to echo across the yard, but she was surprised to hear a soft giggle. Jenn looked up from Pookie's udder and saw her cousin Mimi standing on the porch near Aunty Makiko—well, not *too* near, since Aunty looked like she could breathe fire.

"Hi, Mimi. You came to help fold paper cranes?" What Jenn really wanted to ask was whether Mimi's mother, Aunty Aikiko, was around, too. Jenn hoped Mimi could read her slightly anxious expression.

She could. "I was at my parents' house, and Mom was ranting about something crazy—I thought she mentioned Disneyland, can you believe that?—so when your mom called me to ask if I could help, I drove right over."

Bless her mother. Mom must have called Mimi the second she saw Aunty Makiko had arrived early to harangue Jenn. Out of all the cousins, Mimi was the only one who could manage to sidetrack Aunty Makiko from a tirade.

"Aunty, let's go inside." Mimi laid a hand on the chicken-wing arm, and her voice had modulated subtly to a younger, lighter tone that somehow made Aunty's face a little less strained and lined. "We have a lot of cranes to fold."

But then Aunty's belligerent expression returned. "No, I'll have my say."

Didn't she always?

"Jennifer, you cannot run your own business." She said it like a royal pronouncement.

Squeeze, release, squeeze, release ...

"Jenn, you're squeezing a bit hard," Edward murmured just as Pookie shifted slightly.

"Sorry, Pookie," she told the poor, abused goat. She let go of the two teats and stood to face her aunt. Hopefully her loose jeans hid her quaking thighs. Her entire body shivered as if she were in a strong north wind.

"You don't have experience," Aunty went on. "Why don't you work for Aunty Aikiko to gain some business experience?"

"The only business experience I'd gain would be learning how to run Aunty's restaurant the way Aunty wants it run."

Behind Aunty Makiko, Mimi stifled an amused gasp.

Aunty just about blew a gasket. "This family has done nothing but pamper and support you—"

"This family has never supported me," Jenn shot back. "You only want to use me."

To her surprise, Mimi gave her an encouraging nod.

Aunty's mouth opened and closed like a rather stupid goldfish. Finally, she demanded, "Come here so I can speak to you properly without needing to yell."

"You'll yell whether I'm in front of you or across the bay."

Aunty sputtered.

Jenn turned back to Pookie. "I'm busy. If you want to speak to me, you can do it from there." Hopefully, Aunty wouldn't slip into a pair of the outdoor slippers on the porch and march across the tiny yard.

"Your mother needs you," Aunty said.

"Well, she sees even more of me now than when I was working as a software engineer." Jenn grasped the teats again. "And much more than if I was working for the restaurant."

"Don't you care about Aunty Aikiko? She needs you."

Jenn set her mouth for a moment, then turned to Aunty. "She doesn't need me. Her sons are too lazy or disinclined to take over the restaurant—fine, I understand that. But she has Mimi. She could have trained her daughter, and yet she refuses to. That's her loss." And her own mental hangup. She never valued her only daughter, treating her like something useless.

Mimi had gone slightly pale, but she didn't say anything.

"You are so selfish," Aunty said. "You should care about pleasing your family. You should try to be a good *Japanese* daughter." And here she gave a rather sneering look at Edward.

That prejudiced look fired her blood. No one talked like that to her anymore, and no one talked like that about her friends.

She'd been a people pleaser and a "good Japanese girl" for most of her life, yet her family didn't appreciate her or respect her. Moreover, Aunty was grossly insulting Edward just because he wasn't Asian.

So Aunty didn't like her friend? Jenn would show her how "Japanese" she was.

She turned, grabbed Edward a bit awkwardly around the neck, and kissed him.

The kiss stunned him, dazzled him. The Milky Way exploded in front of his eyes. He felt a hundred feet tall (or at least taller than his normal five foot nine).

And she'd missed his mouth slightly, and her hands around his neck kind of pulled his head at an awkward angle.

But she was only doing this to shock her relatives, who, granted, needed a bit of shocking. Still, this wasn't right, not if he ever wanted a real relationship with Jenn. He grasped her waist to gently push her away.

Makiko's voice grated on his ears. "Yuki! Your daughter is kissing that Hispanic migrant worker!"

His neck tightened. He was actually a Heinz 57 of old world Spanish, Italian, Russian, German, and a little Latvian. But the woman's insulting tone made him grab Jenn's waist and pull her closer instead of pushing her away from him.

Her body melted against him, and an inferno engulfed his head. Holy smokes, she was like his Aunt Lorena's *elote picoso* chiles and corn dish.

Receding footsteps. The *shush* as Makiko yanked open the back door and then a *whoosh! Thump, thump!* as she slammed it shut.

Jenn didn't immediately pull away. That was a good thing, right?

"She's gone, guys," Mimi said.

Jenn backed away, avoiding his eye, her cheeks purple like a plum. "Er ... sorry. I kind of ... lost my temper."

She had pretty good provocation, and he didn't want to make her uncomfortable with him, so he put a light spin on the incident. "You can lose your temper with me anytime."

She flickered a glance up at him, bit her lip, then reluctantly smiled.

"I knew you were going to blow up eventually," Mimi said from the porch.

"I didn't blow up. Do you see any blood and guts?"

Mimi laughed. "Now you sound like me."

Their banter reminded Edward of his own family. It was good to see that Jenn had more than just Trish on her side. After the display today, he'd been afraid she had turned her entire family against her.

She touched his forearm lightly, her eyes pained. "I'm sorry about Aunty."

"Don't be."

Her gaze flickered. "No, really. I'm sorry you had to listen to all that."

"And I'm telling you again, it's okay. My family is even louder, and they've had plenty of fights in front of my friends while I was growing up."

"Really? That's awful." Her eyes were pained again, but it was for him. He wanted to touch her face and maybe brush the blush from her cheeks.

But had she kissed him because of him? Boring Edward Castillo? Or exotic, non-Asian biker Edward who rescued her on a Saratoga road? The doubt made him straighten instead of leaning closer to her. He was glad for Mimi's presence, to keep him in line. "See? We all have crazies in our families."

Jenn ducked her head, hiding her smile. She turned to Mimi. "Thanks for trying to get Aunty away."

"No problem. I owed you anyway."

"For what?"

"For what?" Mimi flung her arms out. "For the reason you're in this mess in the first place. For Brad."

Who was Brad? Suddenly, he wished Mimi gone.

"What do you mean, for Brad? I ruined the party."

"What are you smoking? Brad ruined *your* party. I really didn't know you guys had dated before."

Dated? How long ago? Edward wanted to ask but didn't think he could do it casually without looking like a turd.

Jenn shrugged. "It was a long time ago, in college." But she was tense—he could see the tight set of her shoulders. "Did he ... say anything about that?"

"Oh, I broke up with him." Mimi said it as if she were telling them about the head of cabbage she just bought.

"You did?"

"I figured if he hit *you*, Miss Sweet and Mild, it's almost a guarantee he'll take a swing at me. I mean, with *my* mouth?"

"He hit you?" Edward's question shot out of his mouth, tight with outrage.

"He pushed me." Jenn pulled her hair forward and fiddled with it, the strands framing her face. "It was only once."

"You ripped into him pretty good." Mimi had a rather malicious gleam in her eye. "You might even say he was the catalyst for everything that's happened."

"What do you mean?"

"Well, if you hadn't confronted him, the aunties wouldn't have tried to shut you up, and you wouldn't have gotten mad and decided not to work for Aunty Aikiko, and you wouldn't be forming your own catering business."

Whoa, that was convoluted. But it seemed to be a winding road that had led her to him, so he couldn't complain.

"Speaking of which," Mimi continued, "why do you need to milk that goat if you're forming your own business? You're not going to sell milk, are you?"

"Cheese." Jenn's face had lit up. "I can use goat cheese in one or two dishes for the wedding."

"When's the wedding?" Edward asked. "Trish never mentioned the actual date to me."

"In four weeks."

"And she gave birth the last time I saw you?"

"Yes."

He scratched the back of his head. "You won't be able to use the milk from her for two weeks."

"What? Why?"

"The first two weeks, the goat is producing a special milk for the kid, and it doesn't taste all that great. But after that, you could get maybe a gallon from her a day if you milk her once a day."

"A gallon?" Jenn's eyes narrowed and she stared into space. She reminded him of his uncle when he was calculating harvest dates.

"Doesn't give you much time to make cheese before the wedding," Mimi remarked.

"I'll think of something. What else do I need to know?" she asked him.

They spent more time with Pookie, and even Mimi got a chance to milk her. He explained what Jenn would need to do for milk collection, what equipment she'd need, what precautions she'd need to take with the raw milk.

CHAPTER SIX

After they'd untethered Pookie and let her wander in the tiny yard, Jenn asked Edward and Mimi if they wanted to stay for lunch.

"Your aunty won't mind?" Edward asked.

"She won't stay," Jenn assured him. "She prefers Japanese food, and I always make sure to cook Italian or Mexican when she comes over. In fact, if I start cooking now, it'll chase her out of the house faster."

"Have I mentioned I love the smell of boiling pasta?" Mimi turned toward the back door.

"It's only nine or ten in the morning."

"Remember, I still have to fold cranes with them."

Jenn groaned. "I'll probably have to do that, too. Unless …" She chewed her lip. "I do still have to do a trial run of Trish's wedding cake. Maybe I'll do that this morning."

"So we can have cake for dessert? Bring it on!" Mimi bounced on the balls of her feet as she walked up the steps to the porch.

"What should I do?" Edward asked.

"Do you want to fold cranes?" Jenn asked.

He held out his square, strong hands. "With these?"

Jenn grinned. "Wait for me in the kitchen."

Inside, Edward felt a bit like he was on the deck of the USS *Enterprise*. Everything gleamed with chrome and digital readouts and a few rather nasty-looking knives a Klingon would love.

"Mom!" Jenn's voice sounded high, strained. Through the open doorway of the kitchen, he saw Jenn dart from the hallway into the living room. "Mom, where are my cake pans?"

"In the kitchen." But Mrs. Lim's voice trembled.

"No, my brand-new ones. The special ones I bought for Trish's wedding. The ones that were in the box in my room."

"They're not there?"

A pause. Edward could imagine Jenn counting to three. "I may be getting older, Mother, but I can see well enough to know that the box is empty."

59

Edward actually heard Mrs. Lim gulp. "Er ... well ... do you remember when Aunty Aikiko was here?"

There was a terrible silence.

Edward left the kitchen to go rescue Jenn's mom.

"You let Aunty Aikiko take my cake pans?" Jenn's voice screeched off the low ceiling of the living room just as Edward grasped her shoulders firmly from behind.

"In the kitchen, Jenn," he said.

"You let—"

"They heard you the first time, Jenn." He pitched his voice firmly to cut through her shock and anger. Aunty Makiko looked faintly pleased. "Mimi?" He jerked his head toward the open doorway of the living room as he pulled Jenn backward and out of there.

He managed to zombie-walk her into the kitchen, followed by her cousin. She let out a weak, "I can't believe she let ... They were really expensive ... special order ..."

Edward plopped her onto a barstool next to the island in the middle of the kitchen. "Do you need a glass of water or something?"

"I'll make tea." Mimi bustled around, getting the teapot and mugs.

Jenn stared into space, breathing heavily. "What am I going to do?"

"Retaliate."

"Retaliate?" She turned a confused face to him. "How?"

"Infiltrate and retrieve." He hadn't played all those Xbox games for nothing.

"Retrieve the pans?" Mimi asked. "How?"

"How many people are in your parents' house right now?" he asked Mimi.

"Mom, Dad—no, he might be gone because Mom is going loco. And my four brothers."

"Ages?" He felt like a commando.

"Sixteen, twenty, twenty-four, and twenty-eight."

CHAPTER SIX

Hmm, a bit more formidable than he had expected. "Give me the layout of the house and where the pans might be."

Mimi got a sheet of scratch paper and drew a diagram, putting a star next to the kitchen drawers where the pans would probably be.

"What are you planning?" Jenn asked.

"War," he said with a grin.

CHAPTER SEVEN

J ENN FELT LIKE *Charlie's Angels.*
In honor of the rescue mission, the five cousins and Edward dressed all in black. Trish had showed up with a fire-engine red tube of lipstick, which she made all the girls put on, and sunglasses for everyone, which would obscure their faces but not hamper their aim.

They were armed to the teeth. Each one carried a Super Soaker water gun or water cannon. In fact, Edward had two weapons, including a smaller water gun he'd tucked into his waistband.

They met at Jenn's house and crammed into her SUV. On the way to Aunty Aikiko's house, Edward reviewed the plan with them all.

"Mimi, you're first wave since you'll need to unlock the front door. You said Ryden would probably be in the living room?"

She nodded. "His computer is there. He's always on Facebook® at this time of day."

"He'll give an early warning to the others." Edward grinned. "Good. It'll make it a more interesting fight. Jenn, you're second wave. Head straight into that kitchen to find the pans. Trish, back her up and shoot anyone who tries to stop her. Lex and Venus, you're with me. Once Mimi takes out Ryden, the other boys will come down the stairs to figure out what's going on. We'll have to be ready to take them down."

"Yessir!" Lex said. Her grin was a bit feral.

They parked a few feet away from the house, just out of visual range of the second floor windows. They darted toward the front door, and Mimi shouldered her water cannon in order to slide her house key into the lock. The door unbolted easily. She pushed against it.

It stuck.

Her eyes were frantic. "It's the weather. It makes the wood warp."

Edward positioned himself and whispered to them, "On three. Ready? One, two, three!" He shouldered the door open.

It crashed open with a *bang!* and they rushed inside.

Just their luck, Rick was walking down the stairs as the door flew open. He took one look at them and flipped around, running back upstairs, shouting to his brothers.

In the living room to the left of the door, Ryden sprang up from his chair at the computer and whirled toward them. "What? Mimi?" He saw the water guns. "Oh, no you don't!" He darted toward them, and Mimi shot him with a blast of water from the water cannon.

"Go! Go! Go!" Edward took the stairs two at a time, Lex and Venus behind him. Trish helped Mimi soak her youngest brother while Jenn ran into the kitchen. She yanked open the drawer.

Nothing.

Where would they be? "Mimi!" Jenn whirled. She started pulling open drawers and cabinets.

"Oven!" Mimi shouted from the living room. "Oh, you'll pay for that—"

Suddenly, Aunty Aikiko's shrieking from upstairs sliced through the air. "What are you doing? What's going on?"

Jenn opened the oven door. Nothing inside but some rusty racks.

She pulled on the broiler, but it stuck. She tugged again, straining against it. It groaned open.

There! One of her pans. With a gigantic black spot in the middle. Aunty had burned something in her new pan!

Jenn tucked the pan into the satchel and kept searching. Thumps and bumps rattled the ceiling as the battle waged upstairs.

Mimi and Trish rushed into the kitchen. "Hurry! The boys are forcing Edward, Lex, and Venus down the stairs!"

"Where's Ryden?"

"He ran out the front door, the coward."

Mimi pulled open some cabinets. "Here are two of the pans."

Jenn found the fourth one under the sink. "We've got them all. Let's go!"

They hustled out of the kitchen, slipping a little on the water in the tiled foyer. "Retreat!" Jenn roared up the stairs, where her cousins and Edward were pelting and being pelted by water.

They raced out of the house. Jenn activated the car unlock by remote as they ran, and they scrambled inside, followed by their male cousins.

"Go!" Trish screamed as they clambered inside.

Jenn turned the key even as she slammed the door shut. The engine gunned to life.

The RAV4 screeched away just as the boys reached them, their hands pounding on the windows. Jenn just barely remembered to check for any other cars before pulling into the empty street. She glanced in the rearview mirror and saw the boys standing in the middle of the street, trying to run after them, getting smaller and smaller.

They had done it!

"We did it! We did it!" The cousins screamed and danced in Jenn's kitchen like little girls again. "We did it!"

Jenn pulled Edward into an exuberant hug. His arms tightened around her, and suddenly it was like those movie scenes where the action stops but the camera pans around.

All she heard was the rushing of blood in her ears. All she felt was his solid chest, his strong arms. All she smelled was his musk, with a hint of thyme and verbena.

And then suddenly the movie started playing again.

He loosened his hold on her, releasing one arm to reach into his back pocket. "This calls for a real celebration."

"What do you mean?"

He kept his eyes on her but didn't answer. Instead, he spoke into the phone. "Mama? I'm bringing five beautiful ladies to dinner."

This must be what heaven is like, Jenn thought as Edward's mother embraced her in a paella-scented hug. Mrs. Castillo was short and round with a wide smile and wider arms.

"Welcome, welcome!" She embraced Mimi as well. Venus, Lex, and Trish couldn't make it, but Jenn and Mimi had jumped at the chance to eat Spanish home cooking.

"You're both too skinny! Come, we'll fatten you up. I hope you like Spanish food." Mrs. Castillo kept talking as she led them inside toward the kitchen. "Edward gave me so little notice, so I only made three courses, but I always make a lot of food since we have so many people. You all like Spanish food, yes?" She barely paused for an answer as they entered a gigantic kitchen boasting a huge dining table. "Here is everyone! Let me introduce them all."

People packed the room, adults and children. It reminded Jenn of her own family gatherings except the Castillos seemed to speak in louder voices and laugh louder and longer than her Japanese or Chinese family members.

"We all work on the vineyard and the farm," Edward told her. "These are all my cousins and aunties and uncles. My grandparents passed away several years ago."

"No, no, no." An argument between one of Edward's cousins and an uncle interrupted their conversation.

The swarthy younger man shook his finger at his slender uncle in a gesture that surprised Jenn with its seeming lack of respect. "That fertilizer is useless—"

"It was good enough for Papa—"

"It is outdated. This new one—"

The uncle made a derisive sound. "Fancy and full of filler."

"Argue about fertilizer after dinner," Edward's mama ordered them, as she and several of the aunties set steaming platters of food on the table. She winked at Jenn as she passed. "The men always need something to argue about. It shows they love each other."

Love each other? In Jenn's experience, arguments meant a lack of love, a lack of obedience.

The two men were now smiling and patting each other's shoulders.

Amazing. Did they enjoy the arguments? Or was it something else? Maybe it was how they seemed to so easily agree to disagree. Maybe it was how, despite the fact that they didn't see eye to eye, they still seemed to hold each other in great respect.

Respect. No one in Jenn's family respected her.

"Jenn?" Edward held out a chair for her at the overfilled table.

They all sat, and a hush settled over all of them. The oldest uncle stood. Everyone clasped hands and bowed their heads as he said grace.

It was a prayer similar to others she'd heard before, but here, surrounded by his family and some of hers, it seemed a prayer of community. It reached deep inside her in ways other prayers hadn't before. She could almost feel God's presence.

At the "amen," Edward's hand squeezed hers gently before releasing her.

CHAPTER SEVEN

Dinner was amazing. The paella melted in her mouth. There was also a seafood noodle dish, fideua, and espencat, a mixture of roasted vegetables. The salad had an assortment of spring greens as well as some of the first vine-ripened tomatoes of the summer, juicy jewels that exploded with rich flavor in her mouth.

After dinner, Jenn and Mimi tried to help with the other women clearing and cleaning, but Edward's mama shooed them outside, ordering her son and one of his cousins to show the girls around the vineyard.

They walked through the noisy backyard, where the men were either babysitting—which seemed to involve boisterous games with the children—or sitting and relaxing with an after-dinner glass of wine. They walked along the dirt lanes that crisscrossed the property, coming to the crest of a hill that overlooked the rolling vineyards.

The low-streaming rays of the sun gilded the grape vines, and the acres of rows of plants stretched into the sunset, broken only by a few lanes, a few trees, a few juniper bushes.

"Not all of these vineyards are ours," Edward said, "but most of them."

Faint voices carried to them, and they were joined by the nephew and uncle who had been arguing earlier, again loudly discussing fertilizer. The two men nodded to the foursome before continuing down the lane, intent on their discussion.

Edward smiled after them. "My family is very opinionated, as you can see."

"No one ever gets ... mad?"

He seemed to know she was thinking about her own disagreement with her aunty. "If someone didn't stand up for their opinion, I think we'd be more upset. It's a shame to be too dependent on others for your decisions."

Too dependent on others. Was that what she was? "I'm trying to be more independent."

"I know."

"You do?"

"I do."

It seemed strange that this man would know this after only knowing her for so short a time. He seemed to almost know her better than her own family, but that wasn't possible, was it?

"I guess you've seen me at my worst the past few days," Jenn said. "I hope that you don't think I'm like that all the time."

"No, I can see you're making a bid for independence," he said. "There are always rough spots to iron out."

With her family, with herself. "For the first time, I feel like I have the freedom to think about myself."

"Have you always wanted to please your family?"

"Always. I was always the good cousin." The doormat. The people pleaser. "Now, everything I'm doing is displeasing them." Her job. Her new business. Her new … what was it that was between them? She felt the attraction. She thought he might feel it, too, but she wasn't sure.

"We've gone through a lot together in only a few days," she ventured.

He paused. A long, horrible, excruciating pause from Jenn's point of view, but she knew it was probably only a few seconds. Finally he said with a smile that seemed a bit forced, "Yes, we've become *friends* pretty fast."

She hadn't imagined the emphasis on *friend*.

What did he mean, *friend?* What about that *kiss?* That mind-numbing, hot jalapeno pepper kiss???

Then again, maybe it had only been that way for her. Maybe for him, it had been only, *Eh.*

Suddenly, the wind blew colder than before, and the rays of the sun were dying. The day was over.

They walked back to the house, and Jenn chatted with Edward's cousin while Mimi talked to Edward about his birthday present, the Harley. She overheard him telling her he'd take her for a spin before they left.

She squelched her surge of jealousy, then chastised herself. She'd been almost paralyzed with fear while riding that bike. And now she was begrudging Mimi? What was wrong with her?

She was only a *friend*, that's what was wrong with her. She frowned a little as she glared at Edward's back, following him to the house.

"There you are!" Edward's mama met them in the backyard. "I didn't even get a chance to talk to you at dinner."

"Jenn, why don't you talk to Mama while I take Mimi for a spin on the bike?" Edward suggested.

Mrs. Castillo rolled her eyes. "I don't know why your uncle bought that after I *told* him not to—"

"You worry too much, Mama." Edward bussed his mother on the cheek and led Mimi to a small barn nearby, which had been converted into a garage.

"Edward tells me you've started your own business." Mrs. Castillo sat down on a bench in the backyard, watching a few of the younger cousins playing soccer with the kids.

"I just started my catering business. I'm doing my cousin Trish's wedding in a few weeks."

"How exciting." She smiled at Jenn. "You must be a good cook."

A few weeks ago, she would have said, *I'm only okay*, or *I'm decent*. But why display false modesty? What did it accomplish? It hadn't raised her esteem in her family's eyes, so why bother? "I love to cook. I attended culinary school and got my degree."

Her eyes widened. "Really? How wonderful. So young and so driven. You remind me of my father-in-law, the man who started this winery." She sighed. "His father—my husband's grandfather—didn't approve. Wanted him to raise cows. The old pasture land is down thataway." She gestured toward the rolling foothills south of them.

"He didn't want him to make wine?"

"He didn't want him to be a farmer, working with crops, vulnerable to the weather—an iffy business, in his mind. He wanted him to make money, and at the time, it was in the meat industry. He had his own ideas of what he wanted his son to be."

"Like my family." It slipped out before she could stop herself, but Mrs. Castillo seemed perceptive to the meaning behind her soft words.

"Your family doesn't approve of your new business?"

"That's an understatement. The only ones happy about it are my cousins."

Mrs. Castillo's eyes caught and held hers with gentle firmness. "And is God leading you to form your own business?"

God? Jenn's stomach felt like she'd just stepped off a cliff. Had she even asked God before doing all this?

What did He think of her catering business? Would He be mad at her for not praying about it before quitting her job? Before telling Aunty Aikiko she wouldn't work at the restaurant?

What had she done?

"If you feel God is leading you to form your own business," Mrs. Castillo continued, "your family should not hinder you. Their opinions should not clash with what God wants for you."

"Er …" Jenn's throat had closed up. "I, uh … I didn't exactly ask God … yet."

Mrs. Castillo patted her hand. "Then maybe you should."

And she left it at that.

"Nice goal, Jorge!" she called to one of her nephews, who had just kicked a ball past his much-older cousin.

Jenn stared at the game but saw only a blur of people. What had she done? She'd already quit her job. Had already set the wheels in motion to form her own business. She'd lost the primary source of income of their household besides her mom's retirement.

Maybe she could withdraw her small business loan application? How could she find another job quickly? Would God help her get employment when she'd already run full steam ahead on something that wasn't in His will?

Wait, she didn't know this wasn't His will.
Well, you certainly didn't ask Him, did you?
Could she ask Him now? Would He answer?
Lord … ?
What if it was too late?

CHAPTER EIGHT

SIX MINUTES LATE. On the wedding day, Aunty Aikiko would probably be clocking them down to the second.

"We've got to plate faster," Jenn said, working alongside her sous-chef, Sarah.

Mika, one of the two assistants, passed a plate laden with a petite filet mignon to Karissa, standing at the stove beside her. "Karissa's holding us up." Mika winked and playfully bumped her partner in the hip.

"No, it's Mika." Karissa scooped a delicate piece of fish onto the plate and then spooned the herbed shrimp sauce over the fish.

Jenn took a moment from spooning the red-and-green pasta into the flower-shaped cookie cutter on the plate in front of her—Mimi's idea for a prettier presentation—to study their setup for the trial run of the wedding's entrée plating. It did look like Mika's station was holding things up because she had to spoon the sauce over the fish. "Mika, let's take that sauce and move it here to where Sarah's arranging the vegetable bouquets."

Mika grabbed the pot of sauce and shifted it next to Sarah.

"We'll get a hot pot or something to keep it warm on the day," Jenn said.

"How about a Crock-Pot?" Mimi suggested from where she was doing the last-minute cleanup and presentation of each plate.

"Good idea."

Sarah already had premade bundles of carrots and asparagus artfully tied together with tiny braided raw spinach ropes. She plunked the bundle down on the plate and mimicked spooning sauce over the fish. "That'll work," she said. "I'll still be able to keep up."

"Let's shift the order, then. Mika and Karissa get the plates first, then Sarah, then me, and lastly to Mimi."

They practiced another fifteen minutes before Jenn called a halt. "Good job. We're right on time. We'll get the entire banquet hall served in less than twenty minutes."

The women exchanged high-fives and whoops of delight. Jenn couldn't help the starburst of excitement inside her. She loved this—the precision, the time pressure, the feeling of working as a finely tuned team.

At moments like this, she knew this was what she was made for.

So wouldn't that mean God wanted her to form her own catering business? She still wasn't sure. She'd been praying for over a week and hadn't heard clearly from God. At the back of her mind was a fear that He was mad at her and wasn't speaking to her.

No, that was silly. God wasn't a drama queen teenager.

But how could she know that this path was right for her or not? She needed a sign.

God, please give me a sign. Anything to help me know what Your will is.

Until then, all she could do was prepare for Trish's wedding as best she could. And hope God wouldn't strike her down with lightning. Or worse, send a freak hailstorm to destroy all her Malaysian basil plants. That would certainly answer her question about if this was His will or not.

Mimi nabbed a carrot and crunched it. "One day we'll all work for you in your own restaurant, Jenn."

"I wish," she said.

But Mika, Sarah, and Karissa were nodding as if it were completely possible.

"Why would you want to work in my restaurant? Won't you all want to run restaurants of your own?"

"I need to learn all your secrets first." Sarah winked.

"It's too much work," Mimi said. "Remember, I've seen firsthand how to run a restaurant."

"That's flattering, guys, but I need to crawl before I can walk." A restaurant of her own—she'd love it. The freedom to create her own dishes, to change the menu anytime she wanted, to experiment. Suddenly, that dream didn't seem so far-fetched because she wasn't chained to Aunty Aikiko's restaurant. But first she needed to get this catering business off the ground. "Let's practice the appetizers really quickly."

"Won't most of that already be premade?" Mimi asked.

"Yes, and we'll only have to pop them into the oven in timed batches. But I want to practice so Sarah can get the timing and frying temperature down for the Asian popcorn chicken, and so I can see how many of the French savory pastries we can get done for each of her batches."

"I know the Malaysian basil isn't quite ready yet," Sarah said, "and we'll be practicing with regular basil for today, but can we do a batch or two with a little Malaysian basil? I don't know if it'll wilt differently from regular."

"Good point. I'll go out and get some." Jenn took off her apron and headed out the back door.

The sunlight greeted her, but her thoughts were still stormy. What if she was going about this all wrong? What if God wanted her to work for Aunty Aikiko? Really, would it be that bad?

Yes, it would be that bad. She'd be a drudge, and Aunty would be able to treat her that way because Jenn was family. Jenn wouldn't have any outlet for her creativity, just overseeing the same dishes week after week, month after month, year after year.

One of the goat kids left off playing with his (her?) sibling and approached Jenn. Aw, how cute, it wanted to come to her …

No, it bypassed her completely, instead traveling around the side of the porch toward the gate guarding the basil plants.

It was then that she noticed sounds coming from the side of the house. Suspicious sounds. Like plastic pots being crunched by goat hooves.

The basil!

Jenn bounded off the porch and turned the corner.

The gate to the basil was open. Unlatched.

And Pookie stood in the midst of a chaos of overturned pots, contentedly munching on a Malaysian basil plant.

Aunty Aikiko had gotten her ultimate revenge.

Jenn supposed she deserved it after attacking Aunty's home with a stealth infantry armed with water cannons.

"I'm sorry," Mom moaned, sinking into the living room sofa. "I didn't see anything wrong with letting Aikiko look at the basil. I watched her very carefully while she was in there."

"It's not your fault, Mom." Jenn dropped onto the sofa next to her parent. "It would have been rude to refuse her."

They sat there, side by side, in silence. Jenn felt like she had the one time when she discovered the dog really had eaten her homework, a cake for one of her high school home economics classes.

Like a CSI, Jenn had examined the gate. No sign of forced entry. Meaning it had been left unlatched when Aunty Aikiko left.

Jenn had also found the shred of a Snickers bar wrapper caught at the base of the gate frame. Mom had confirmed that Aunty had been eating a Snickers bar, but hadn't paid attention to where she put it. Jenn speculated that Aunty had cracked the gate open with the half-eaten candy stuck between the gate and the fencing. It was doubtful Mom would have even noticed.

"I'm sorry, Jenn," Mom said again. "I know I was shocked and dismayed when you decided not to work for Aunty, but you have been so much happier for the past few weeks." She sighed. "I can't tell you to not do something you enjoy and which you're good at. I know you'd have hated working for Aunty."

A feeling like an airy Shetland shawl settled on Jenn's shoulders. She put her arm around her mom and squeezed gently. "Did you have fun with Max last night?"

"It was wonderful. I haven't been to a sock hop in ages." She yawned. "We shouldn't have stayed so late, though."

"You should get ready for your breakfast meeting with the *Obon* dance planning committee." Jenn rose from the sofa. She was glad Mom had the meeting at the San Jose Buddhist temple to keep her occupied. Otherwise, she'd probably have wandered around the house, worrying and regretting what had happened with Jenn's basil. "I have to go milk Pookie."

She was trying really hard not to blame the poor goat. After all, it wasn't Pookie's fault that evil Aunty Aikiko had dangled the temptation of a Snickers bar *and* a forbidden Eden of Malaysian basil in front of the poor animal. No goat in her right mind could have resisted.

But the remembered scene of destruction still gave Jenn a pang in her heart.

Well, she'd wanted a sign. This was as good a sign as any, wasn't it? She should just go groveling to Aunty Aikiko today, begging for her to give her a job at the restaurant. Or maybe God wanted Jenn to try to get another job as a software programmer?

Either way, it looked like God had closed the door on her catering business. She could do Trish's marinated popcorn chicken with regular basil, but it wouldn't taste the same. The Malaysian basil gave it a very distinct, delicious flavor. The demolition of all the special basil she'd spent weeks cultivating—and that stuff didn't grow easily in Silicon Valley, that was for sure—seemed like a banner in the sky from God.

Or a punishment for Jenn stepping out of God's will.

But a part of her knew God didn't punish people that way. She wasn't thinking clearly. She had to get back to her daily Bible reading, to her prayer time, to find out what God really wanted for her life. Better late than never, right?

Pookie seemed a bit remorseful as she stood at tether for Jenn to milk her.

"I guess it's okay," Jenn groused to her goat as she began to milk. "It's not your fault you were born as a *bottomless pit.*"

Pookie bleated softly and chomped on her bucket of goat feed.

A strong smell wafted up to her. Not unpleasant, just … different.

Jenn scanned the area around her and the goat. What was that smell? Where was it coming from? It was a very strong, nutty scent. Almost like a Snickers bar.

Snickers.

She stopped milking, picked up the bucket, and sniffed. It was definitely the milk.

But Pookie had eaten only one Snickers bar and probably only part of it since Mom had said Aunty had been eating it.

Was it the basil?

She couldn't think of what else could make the goat milk smell so strongly different.

She sniffed again. Yes, definitely nutty, with herbal overtones and maybe even a hint of hot pepper.

She finished milking and brought the milk inside the house. She didn't particularly like the taste of raw goat milk, but she poured a little into a glass to taste it.

It reminded her of hazelnuts. But not quite hazelnut milk or almond milk. There was an exotic herbal flavor underlying the nuttiness that would pair really well with fish. Maybe salmon …

Salmon? *She* was the nutty one. It was just a weird-tasting batch of goat milk.

That was unlike anything she'd ever tasted before.

A rising rumbling in her chest, like an ocean wave about to crash magnificently on the shore.

She was a chef now. And she'd just discovered a completely new flavor.

"Oh. My. Goodness." Venus actually dropped her fork onto the plate, she was so stunned by Jenn's new dish.

Jenn stared anxiously at Venus. "That means it's good, right? Not that it's so bad you want to puke?"

Jenn knew that Venus, who had dined at all the top-star restaurants in San Francisco because of her job as chief technology officer at her company, knew good food.

Her reaction must mean it was *really* good food.

Right?

Venus took another bite of the salmon, dressed in a light cream tomato sauce using goat's milk, with hazelnuts and almonds and slivers of (regular) basil on top. Her eyes closed blissfully as she chewed. "Jenn, that is the best thing you've ever made. And that includes the peanut butter cups."

Wow. Even the Grand Marnier lava cake hadn't gotten that kind of endorsement. "Edward?" she asked shyly. She had asked him over ostensibly to ask if Pookie would be okay after eating all that basil and had casually asked him to taste her new dish, too. The truth was, even as a friend, she had wanted to see him, and Pookie was as good an excuse as any without making her look too desperate.

He chewed thoughtfully. "You did a good job using just enough goat milk for the sauce to bring out the flavor but not too much to overpower it. If you had more goats, more time, and more basil, you could make cheese to crumble over it, too."

"That's what I was thinking." Jenn leaned close in excitement and caught a whiff of his musk and that hint of thyme. "I can't do it for the wedding, but I can offer this dish for future events. I'd have to alter the sauce a bit if I use cheese, too, though."

His dark eyes captured hers. "Amazing." And for a moment, she didn't think he meant the dish.

Friend. He'd said *friend* deliberately.

She straightened and turned to the bride-to-be. "Trish? What do you think?"

Her other cousin was lost in her own world, shoveling salmon into her mouth.

"Trish?"

She started and looked up. "Can I lick my plate? Would that be gross?"

Venus gave Jenn a high five over the kitchen table. "You outdid yourself. You seriously could open a restaurant with this dish."

A restaurant. Her own place. An empty canvas for her creativity to create unique dishes.

No, hadn't she learned anything? "I'd have to pray about that. And God would have to really give me the go-ahead for me to do something like that."

"Have you been praying about your catering business?" Trish helped herself to more salmon.

"I think ..." Jenn was still cautious about voicing her dreams, in case she hadn't been hearing from God clearly. "I think He does want me to do this. The Malaysian basil goat milk was a really fortunate accident."

"But you don't have any more basil, right?" Venus asked.

"Actually, I googled it a few days ago—right after I discovered about the goat milk—and found out that a day spa in Sonoma has released a product using Malaysian basil extract as its main ingredient. I e-mailed the dermatologist researcher to ask her about her plants, and she called me. I told her about Pookie and the wedding, and she offered to let me take a few dozen plants in exchange for me cooking dinner one night for her family."

"So you can make this for the wedding?" Trish had already finished her second helping.

"I think so. I don't need much of the goat's milk for the sauce. If I can get two gallons off of Pookie the two days before the wedding, I'll have enough."

"Hooray!" Trish wiggled in a happy dance while sitting in her chair. "Can I have more?"

Jenn pushed the platter toward her. "But the goat's milk discovery isn't the only reason why I think God wants me to form my own catering business. My employees"—it seemed so professional to call them employees!—"are working out really well. We're a good team. We're almost like a family."

"Even Mimi?" Trish asked, a bit skeptical.

"Mimi's been great. She's great in the kitchen—and after helping Aunty at the restaurant for so many years, it's no wonder. She also has a great eye for presentation, and she's had great ideas."

Jenn took a deep breath. "And if those things weren't enough, I've been praying a lot. And I feel a weird sort of peace when it comes to my business. I think God is saying this is what He wants me to do."

The look Edward gave her was a warm ocean swell, washing over her, buoying her up, surrounding her completely. "I'm glad, Jenn. I've been praying for you, too."

A man who prayed. She really couldn't think of anything more attractive.

They helped Jenn wash up, and then Trish suggested a movie. "My mom has Elyssa, so I'm free all afternoon."

"I can't." Jenn put the rinsed frying pan in the dish rack. "I have to pick up Mom from Japantown in about an hour."

"Japantown?" Trish frowned. "I saw her there yesterday."

Hmm. That was strange. Jenn shrugged. "She was out of the house early this morning and said she'd need me to pick her up this afternoon at three."

At that moment, her cell phone rang. "Oh, it's Mom. Hello?"

"Jenn?" The voice quavered.

"Mom? What's wrong?" Did she get mugged or something? Why did she sound so scared?

"I need you to pick me up."

"Sure. Where are you? The Asian supermarket? Or the *mochi* shop?"

"I'm at the oncologist's office."

Plunk. That was Jenn's stomach splattering on the floor. "You told me you were going to Japantown." Her voice was strained, high.

It made Trish, Venus, and Edward all glance at her with concerned looks. Trish silently mouthed, *What's wrong?*

"I didn't want to worry you. The doctor called this morning and asked me to come in."

Mom had had a routine exam last week. "What about?"

"Jenn." Her voice was soft now, thready. "The cancer's back."

CHAPTER NINE

EDWARD RUSHED TO catch her as her legs collapsed under her. She shook violently in his arms, but her hand clenched the cell phone. "Are they sure? Are they sure it's back?"

Venus gasped and turned white. She glanced at Trish. "Her mom's cancer," she whispered.

The word was like an iron claw twisting his heart. He'd lost Papa a few years ago, but the grief still burst upon him every so often, shredding his soul. It had been horrible watching him die so slowly.

"Mom, calm down." Jenn swallowed, her eyes frantic but not seeing anything in front of her. "Don't worry. We'll get the money somehow."

But her voice broke slightly, as if only a thread of willpower held her back from hysterical sobbing. She sagged against him, barely standing on her own legs. Barely aware he held her.

"Okay. Bye." The cell phone clattered to the kitchen floor.

Edward maneuvered her to a stool next to the island in the middle of the kitchen. She swayed, and he held out his arms warily, wondering if she were going to pass out.

"Jenn?" Trish touched her shoulder, and Jenn started.

82

"It's back," she whispered.

"We heard," Venus said gently.

"I feel like I've been dunked in ice water," she said, her teeth starting to chatter.

"It's the shock," Venus told her.

"I can't feel my feet. Or my hands. Or my head." Jenn shivered once violently. "But there's so much I need to do. See how much we have in savings. Call Mom's insurance company. The premium is so high ... They raised their rates ..."

Venus clenched Jenn's hand tightly. "Don't worry about that now. We'll help you through this."

Jenn nodded, but dumbly. "I need to go pick her up from the doctor's office. Her boyfriend drove her there this morning, but he's working right now."

"You're not driving anywhere." Edward was surprised at how forceful his voice came out. "I'll drive your car for you. Just tell me where to go."

She looked at him for the first time since receiving the phone call. Her eyes frightened him—like the dark cave entrance into a tomb. "Thanks." She still wasn't quite present with them, still in shock.

"Don't worry about the money," Venus told her. "I can lend you whatever you need."

Jenn shook her head. "We borrowed from you last time."

"And you paid me back."

"But this time ..." She swallowed hard. "I have no job." And finally a tear fell, but she clumsily brought a hand up to swipe it away. She stood up, and although she wasn't completely stable, she seemed able to walk. "I have to go pick up Mom."

"We'll come with you," Trish said.

Jenn shook her head. "Where will Mom sit?" And she walked out of the kitchen, followed by Edward.

He drove her in silence to the doctor's office in Palo Alto. He didn't know what to say. All the things that came to mind sounded stupid or shallow or presumptuous, especially since he'd been so obvious when he had told her he wanted to be her *friend*.

It hadn't been true. He'd wanted to be much more than a friend, but he also hadn't been sure that she wasn't with him only to spite her family. He'd been afraid of being hurt, so he'd deliberately distanced himself from her.

He'd been a moron.

And now, when she needed someone, he had forfeited any right to comfort her or help her. All he could do was drive the stupid car for her.

"Stop worrying," she suddenly said. "You don't have to say anything to me."

Had she been reading his mind?

"After all, what can anybody say? And the silence is what I need right now." She leaned her head against the seat and closed her eyes.

He expected the rest of the ride to be quiet, but she almost immediately spoke. "I've failed."

"You haven't failed anybody," he responded hotly.

"Yes, I—"

"I know exactly what you're feeling. I lost my father to cancer a few years ago."

The silence was heavy with emotion.

"I should have listened to my family," Jenn finally said. "I should have been a good daughter. What was the point in striking out on my own when all I've done is bring stress on my mom?"

"You couldn't have known this would happen. You said you felt God wanted you to do this."

"Maybe I misheard God. Maybe I only heard what I wanted to hear."

"All this is still not your fault."

"My head tells me it's not my fault," Jenn said. "But I can't help feeling that I've failed Mom. I've failed God."

"You can't fail God," Edward said. "Love never fails."

84

"I don't love Him enough. I didn't even ask Him before I told my Aunty off."

"You don't need to love him 'enough.' He loves you enough for a thousand lifetimes."

She closed her eyes, then, and the tears started falling thick and fast, but silently.

"You tried to please your family. And then you broke away and tried to please yourself." Edward couldn't seem to make his mouth stop. "But through it all, God still loves you."

"I don't know what to do."

"You do your best to please God," he said. "He'll take care of the rest." He had to believe that. He had seen it in his own pain. He had to believe it for her, too. Maybe his own belief, his own prayers, would somehow help her through this storm.

"I don't know what God wants." She sighed, but it came out like a sob. "The walls are closing in. I don't have any other options." She took a deep breath that sounded as if it caused her pain. "I have to ask Aunty Aikiko for a job," she said in a small voice.

No, that just seemed wrong. "There has to be another way."

And a niggling idea formed in his mind. But a still voice inside him seemed to caution him. Jenn had jumped without asking God. Edward shouldn't, either.

"She can offer me a job right away." Jenn swallowed hard. "A paycheck right away. What's my pride in the face of Mom's health?"

He couldn't answer her. He had a million things he wanted to say but kept his mouth closed. If he could figure something out, he'd tell her.

Until then, he'd pray.

Before Jenn could unlock her front door, Trish opened it. "Hi, Aunty Yuki," Trish greeted Jenn's mom.

"Oh, hello, Trish." Mom's voice hadn't lost that reedy tone.

"I'll leave you now," Edward said, touching Jenn's shoulder.

She wanted him to stay. He was like a buoy in a choppy bay. But he was only a *friend*. And he was probably busy. And she had too many things she needed to do. "Thanks for driving."

"I'll call you," he said in a firm voice.

It surprised her into meeting his gaze, which held hers. His voice had almost sounded like a promise.

And then he was gone.

Trish had made tea for Mom, but she shook her head. "I think I want to take a nap."

Trish and Jenn tucked her into bed. Jenn wanted to curl up in bed, too. Except all the same demons would be waiting for her when she woke up. Better to face them now.

"Where's Venus?" Jenn asked Trish as they returned to the kitchen. She drank some of the tea Mom had refused.

"Her work called. She didn't want to go, but I made her, since I was staying here."

Jenn let the porcelain cup warm her fingers. She was still cold.

No, she didn't have time to feel sorry for herself. She went to pick up the cordless phone.

"What are you doing?" Trish demanded.

"I have to call Mom's insurance." Jenn searched for the number among the cards and papers taped to the refrigerator.

"Not now." Trish grabbed the phone from her. "We're going for a walk."

"I can't leave Mom."

"She's not a toddler. You can leave her asleep in the house for a few minutes."

Trish bullied Jenn into putting on her tennis shoes.

"You should be with your daughter," Jenn grumbled.

"She's napping at my mom's" was Trish's unruffled answer.

They walked to the nearby park. When Trish tried to stop them at a bench, Jenn pressed on. She didn't want to talk. She wanted to do something. She *had* to do something or she'd shatter into a million shards of glass.

But Trish grabbed her and plopped her down on the bench like a rag doll.

"Trish," Jenn protested.

"You're not getting away from me. You're not getting away from God."

"What are you talking about?" Jenn slumped in the seat.

Trish sat primly beside her. "I was praying while you were gone."

"Thanks," Jenn mumbled.

"And I kept feeling this urge to take you to this park. To sit you on this bench. And to just wait."

"Wait for what?" She didn't want to play games, not when Trish was in her ultra-spiritual mode.

"You tell me." And Trish shut her mouth and stared at the trees.

This was stupid. Jenn fiddled with a loose thread on her jeans. She'd already said it all to God while in the car with Edward. God was probably tired of listening to her.

But have you listened to Me?

The words welled up in her, bubbling up from a deep, secret place inside her.

She had nothing to say in reply.

The bench faced an empty playground, and beyond that, a line of redwood trees. A faint breeze fingered through her hair.

It was quiet here. Despite the breeze, there was a strong stillness over everything. Even the birdsong was muted.

Be still and know that I am God.

And so she did.

She emptied her racing thoughts. She listened to the hushed gossip of the tree branches high overhead.

And then Trish started to sing.

Jenn knew the song. "Every Time I Breathe" by Big Daddy Weave.

She breathed deep, smelling the faint musk of the redwoods, the tang of freshly mowed grass.

And as Trish sang, suddenly Jenn felt the presence of God.

Not a physical presence. But she knew they weren't alone. And it felt like a hand cupped her aching, throbbing heart with coolness. Stillness.

Trish's song grew louder. She was completely unashamed. She was opening herself up, baring herself to Jesus, who was somehow right there with them—a soft presence, and yet a powerful presence. A presence that made Jenn feel small.

But loved.

Small and loved. And suddenly that didn't seem so small.

The God who grew the redwoods above them, whose breath stirred the light breeze, loved her. And if He loved her, He'd take care of her.

Life was hard. But God would take care of her.

It seemed such a simple realization. Almost trite. But in light of Trish's gusty singing—her vulnerability that seemed to reflect the light of Jesus's face—it was a natural thing for Jenn to understand after all that had happened today. Over the past several weeks, actually.

She started singing along with Trish, softly at first. But that seemed rude, when Jesus was baring His heart to her.

So she sang louder. She sang from her heart. And when they sang the last line of the chorus, the words vibrated through her bones: "And I am so in love with You."

Jesus, please help me figure out what to do now.

A soft answer: *It'll be okay.*

Before, Jenn had always needed to down a chocolate truffle or two before calling Grandma. It was her version of liquid courage.

CHAPTER NINE

She wasn't sure if it was her recent rebellious phase or if she was still in shock over Mom's sickness, but her heartbeat didn't even blip above normal resting rate as she dialed Grandma's phone number.

"Hello?"

"Hi, Grandma, it's Jenn."

"Hello, Jenn, how are you doing?"

How strange that after the irritated reception she'd received from her other relatives, Grandma actually seemed a bit friendlier than normal.

Not that Jenn had ever had a bad relationship with Grandma. Unlike Lex or Venus, she and Trish tended to strive to please Grandma Sakai rather than antagonize her. Jenn usually went to extremes in order to avoid becoming an object of Grandma's wrath, so she rarely heard Grandma scold or nag her for anything.

Still, Grandma's almost *friendly* tone put her more on edge than if she'd barked, "What do you want?" into the phone.

Jenn swallowed. "I'm okay, but I have some bad news about Mom."

A beat of silence. "The cancer is back?"

"Yes." Jenn took a long, slow breath. "Can you please tell the aunties and uncles? Trish and Venus were with me when I got the news."

"I'm so sorry, Jenn." There was a rich compassion in Grandma's voice that made tears rush into Jenn's eyes. "I'll come over in a few minutes."

"Thanks, Grandma." She hung up the phone just as Mom walked into the kitchen. "How are you feeling?"

Mom's face crumpled and she just shook her head.

"Grandma's coming over." Jenn fumbled for what to say. "Um ... are you hungry?"

Mom came up to her and put her hands on Jenn's cheeks. "Sweetheart, I'm so sorry."

"Mom! This isn't your fault."

"No, I'm sorry for not telling you about Max. I'm sorry for being so unsupportive of your catering business. I'm sorry for letting Aunty

89

Aikiko push you around. And now you have to give up your dreams again to take care of me."

"Mom, I love you. I would do anything for you." It had been just the two of them for so long. What would Jenn do without her?

"You always do anything anybody asks of you." Mom's voice rose in pitch and strength. "Always. No one ever does anything for *you*."

She wasn't sure if Mom was getting mad at herself or Jenn or someone else. "Mom, you do plenty for me."

"I'm tying you down. I'm keeping you from what you want to do."

"No, Mom, I'm tying *you* down." The pain in her mother's voice strummed the pain in her chest. "About Max—I didn't want things to change, but I wasn't thinking about your needs, just mine."

"Why shouldn't you care about your own needs for once?" Mom said on a sigh.

"It's one thing to be more independent. It's another to be completely selfish."

A beat of silence, then both of them said at the same time, "I'm sorry."

Identical chuckles from daughter and mother, then a gentle hug.

"You won't be alone, Mom. You have me, and Max ..." Would he stick around once the treatments started? Would they take a toll on the relationship?

Apparently Mom had her doubts, too, because she shrugged. "Who knows how that will turn out?"

"Let me make you some tea." Jenn got up to get the green tea from the cabinet.

They sat in silence while the water boiled, and then the doorbell rang. Jenn opened it to Grandma, who surprised her by giving her an awkward hug. "Are you okay?" she asked Jenn.

"Yes," she said automatically.

Grandma paused, an unusually hesitant catch of her breath.

Jenn had never seen her this way. She was always so confident.

"Are you really?" Grandma asked.

Jenn avoided her gaze. "Mom's health is the most important thing right now."

Grandma let that pass. She headed toward the kitchen. "I told your mother's siblings, and I asked them not to call you right now."

"Thanks, Grandma."

Mom made an effort to pull herself together as they entered the kitchen.

"Grandma, can I get you some tea?" Jenn pulled out another cup just as the telephone rang.

She considered not answering, but the incessant ringing set her teeth on edge, so she picked up. "Hello?"

"Jenn, it's Aunty Aikiko."

Why in the world was she calling? Hadn't Grandma told her not to?

"I'm sorry, Aunty Aikiko, Mom can't talk to anyone right now." She used Aunty's full name and raised her eyebrows at Mom, just in case Mom wanted to talk to her. She shook her head at Jenn.

Grandma's brow darkened. She marched over to the phone and stabbed the speaker button but didn't say anything.

"I don't want to talk to your mom. I want to talk to you," Aunty said.

"What about?" Jenn asked. Maybe Aunty was offering to help them in some way?

"I heard the news. I'm very sorry." Aunty actually did sound a bit subdued.

"Thank you."

Aunty's voice then took on a more businesslike crispness. "I'm assuming you're finally giving up that silly idea about your catering business? After all, you can't enter into a risky venture like that when your mother is ill."

Jenn pressed her lips together and glared at the phone. "Yes." The word came out strangled. She didn't want to do this. She had to do this, for Mom.

"I'm also assuming you'll get another job to help pay for her medical bills?"

Not an offer of help. An offer of indentured servitude. "Yes."

"Well, I can offer you a job that'll start right away," Aunty said briskly.

Here was the moment. She had known, in the back of her mind, that she had to make this choice. She had to find a regular job with health insurance benefits, or they would never be able to afford Mom's treatments. But this moment seemed to have come too soon. She wasn't ready to make this sacrifice. She just wasn't ready.

Well, when would she be ready?

Jenn had to do this. Even if she called a recruiter this moment, there was no guarantee she'd be able to get a job within the next month or two, and it was unlikely they'd be very sympathetic when she said she had to take time off to help her mom. Aunty, on the other hand, would let Jenn have a flexible schedule.

This was the only way to make sure Mom would be able to get the treatments she needed. This was the only way to be able to take time off to take Mom to the doctor's and hospital visits.

And working for Aunty wouldn't be the death of her dreams. It would be hard to untangle herself from the restaurant later, in a few years, but Jenn had grown a backbone in the past few weeks. Surely she could regrow it later, stand up to Aunty, and quit work at the restaurant—when Mom's health was better. So while this was a hard decision, it wasn't hopeless, surely?

So why did she feel like she'd stepped off a cliff to fall into a dark abyss?

Now she was being silly. Aunty's restaurant wasn't a dark abyss. Just … an Asian version of *Hell's Kitchen*.

A raging headache started beating against the back of her eyeballs. She had to turn away from the phone, biting her knuckles for a moment to calm herself, to gather the courage to do what she had to do.

She took a deep breath. "Thank you, Aunty. Yes, I'll work for you."

There was a surprised pause, then a triumphant "Wonderful."

"Yes." As wonderful as a slug in the middle of a chocolate cake.

"I'm so pleased. I'm just glad you realized you made a mistake in not coming to work for me the first time."

She almost said yes. The old Jenn would have said yes. But while she was going to work for Aunty after all, she wasn't the old Jenn, and Aunty better figure that out right away. "No, I didn't make a mistake. I think God did want me to quit my job and start my own catering company. It's taught me a lot about myself and my faith." She'd never had the courage to speak so openly about Christianity with them before. She thought she'd feel more nervous, but she felt a strange calm. "I also love my mother, and sometimes God asks us to make sacrifices. We need money to pay for her treatments and the insurance premium. And you were generous enough to offer me a job that starts right away. So I'm accepting. For Mom's sake."

But this time, she wasn't doing it to please her family. She was doing this because she loved Mom and she wanted to please God. And even though dread slushed around in her stomach like a mountain of worms, she knew this was the right thing to do. She knew this was what God wanted her to do. She knew more certainly than anything else she'd ever known in her entire life.

Suddenly, Grandma reached out and punched the speaker button again.

"Grandma, you just hung up on her."

"I know."

Grandma had a calm face as usual, but there was something different about her eyes. They were wider, more tense. She looked almost stunned.

Well, Aunty did go against what Grandma had told her about calling them today. Flouting orders wasn't an everyday occurance in the Sakai family.

Grandma then did a really strange thing. She placed her hand on Jenn's cheek.

Grandma wasn't big on affection. As in, she never did it aside from an occasional hug. The touch of her cool hand on Jenn's skin turned her into a statue. If she moved, Grandma's hand would fall away.

"You are a *good* girl, Jennifer." Her grandmother's voice was strange, too. Emphatic. Low and throbbing. Affirming.

Then her hand dropped away, and it was as if a dream dissipated and real life rushed in.

Mom sat at the island in the middle of the kitchen, an utterly astonished expression on her drawn face, but she didn't dare say a word to Grandma, didn't ask why or what. It just wasn't done.

Grandma eased herself into a chair next to Mom. "How are you feeling?" she asked in a normal voice. It was as if the moment had never happened.

Jenn touched a fingertip to her cheek.

She went about making something for them to eat. It was too early for dinner, but she knew Mom hadn't eaten lunch, so she panfried a few small salmon filets and poured her new goat's milk sauce over it, garnishing it with ribbons of fresh basil.

A part of her nagged that food didn't magically make anything better. But Mom's tired eyes followed her as she prepared and fried the salmon, one of her favorites, and Jenn hoped it might cheer her up a little. After all, wasn't good food a pleasure? They'd had enough of pain today.

She served the dishes with angel hair noodles tossed lightly with some homemade pesto she'd pulled out of the freezer, presenting it with a bit of a flourish.

"How lovely. Thank you, Jenn," Mom said.

"I'm not very hungry," Grandma said, although she eyed the dish as if she might be induced to change her mind.

So Jenn said, "It's a new recipe. I'd love to know what you think, Grandma."

Grandma took one bite and went completely still.

Jenn blinked and stared at her. She wasn't sure if her reaction was good or bad. She didn't spit it out, so that was good, right? And Venus and Trish and Edward had liked it. It couldn't be awful. But maybe Grandma didn't like the slight tang of the goat's milk. Maybe it was too strange for her. Maybe ...

"This is new?"

Jenn nodded. "A light tomato cream sauce with nuts."

"Jenn, this is the most amazing dish I've ever eaten."

Bam! Jenn's world tilted, then righted itself. She grabbed at the marble countertop of the island. "Really?"

"You are ... brilliant."

Wow, two superlatives in the space of a minute. Maybe this wasn't really Grandma and some virus had taken over her body to turn her into a flesh-eating zombie. Who liked salmon with tomato cream sauce.

"T-thanks."

Mom tried the dish at Grandma's words, and her eyes lit up. "Oh my, this is wonderful, sweetheart." Which she said about everything Jenn cooked. Well, except for the one time she'd mistakenly added a tablespoon of cayenne pepper instead of a teaspoon and Mom had been crying too much to say anything about the dish.

"I saw your small business loan application," Grandma said without stopping eating.

Not surprising, considering she owned the bank. Jenn figured she had a good chance of getting it, except ... "I don't need it anymore."

Grandma's mouth tightened slightly, then she abruptly smiled. "With dishes like this, I can see why you wanted to form your own business. One day you'll be a success, Jenn."

Grandma's approbation floored her. And warmed her. And made the day suddenly not so horrific. "Thanks, Grandma." She'd think about all this someday later, when the clouds over them weren't pouring a rain of misery.

Grandma's eyes suddenly flickered in the light from the glass pane in the back door, and her brow puckered. She blinked.

"Jenn, is that a goat in your backyard?"

CHAPTER TEN

J ENN WAS NEVER going to eat teriyaki ever again.

She plated another beef teriyaki, followed by two plates of chicken teriyaki and two plates of salmon teriyaki, and set them on the counter for the waitresses to deliver to their customers.

She tried to tell herself that teriyaki was the mainstay of any Japanese restaurant. That it kept the restaurant in business. That it was a low-fat, tasty way to cook various meats.

Except that the smell also coated the inside of her nostrils so that every breath was teriyaki. The sticky sauce somehow got everywhere, including in her hair. And the vats of dark, premade teriyaki sauce reminded Jenn of things best left unsaid.

She'd lived a week of pure torture. Every minute, she'd had to remind herself of why she needed to be here. She closed her eyes and envisioned Mom's pale face. She remembered how Aunty Aikiko hadn't batted an eye when Jenn told her when she had to take off work to drive Mom to the doctor's office. She remembered the cost estimates the doctor had thoughtfully given to her at their last visit.

New orders came in—a salmon teriyaki, two beef teriyaki platters, and a bowl of udon noodles, which would have been a nice change for

Jenn, if only mentally, except that the clear udon broth also smelled like teriyaki to her.

"Mom!" Aunty Aikiko's panicked voice cut through the busy noises of the kitchen. "Mom! You can't go back there!"

"Oh, *can't* I?" Grandma's steely voice held more menace, although it was only half the volume of Aunty's.

Grandma entered the kitchen, her eye scanning the shocked faces until she saw Jenn. She waved an imperious hand. "Come here, Jenn. You're leaving right now."

"What?" Jenn almost dropped the bowl of udon noodles.

"What?!" Aunty Aikiko screeched.

"We'll discuss this outside," Grandma said. "I can't hear myself think in here." Which was rather odd because for once the kitchen was quiet, everyone paused in shocked silence.

"Mom," Aunty Aikiko said, trying to regain her composure. "Jenn's working—"

"Not anymore." Grandma grabbed Jenn forcibly by the wrist and tugged.

The udon bowl tipped, and broth went everywhere.

Well, no, not everywhere in the kitchen. Just everywhere Jenn was.

The porcelain bowl hit the floor and shattered amid a nest of noodles. The hot soup took a moment to soak through her apron and into her clothes, stinging her skin. She fumbled with the knot of her apron ties while trying to make her body shrink away from her clothes. "Owowowow!"

She could have sworn a noodle slithered into her underwear.

She got the apron off, but her jeans were still soaked and sticking hotly to her legs, noodles had found their way into her shirt collar and some hung down the front of her shirt, and her bra felt like she'd put it in the microwave for a minute before putting it on.

Grandma paused, then said, "See? She can't cook while wearing somebody's lunch. She's leaving now." She grabbed Jenn's wrist again, and Jenn allowed herself to be towed out of the kitchen.

"Mom …" Aunty Aikiko followed them, her pointy-toed shoes kicking Jenn in the Achilles tendons.

Jenn's wet shoes slipped on the slick floor of the dining area, and she did a half-split before righting herself.

Grandma glanced back—not at Jenn but at Aunty. "Aikiko, my bank holds the lease on this building."

Just that one sentence, and Aunty stopped following them. Jenn looked back and saw Aunty standing bewildered, angry, frustrated. The waitresses never stopped their busy movements, but they gave her a wide berth.

Then Grandma's hand on her wrist tugged her along, and she had no choice but to follow.

They erupted from the restaurant into the sunlight beating down on the streets of San Jose Japantown.

"Come." Grandma led her to where she'd miraculously found street parking close to the restaurant. "We're going to the bank."

"The bank" meaning Grandma's bank, founded by Grandpa Sakai and made significantly successful after he'd married Grandma, who now ran it after his death.

"I need to change—"

"I have some spare clothes at the bank."

"That'll fit me?" Jenn eyed Grandma, who was a good six inches shorter.

"Mimi left them a few months ago by accident, and I never got around to giving them back to her. I'm sure they'll fit you."

Jenn wasn't sure if she should be flattered Grandma thought Jenn would fit into twentysomething Mimi's skintight jeans, or if she should admit to Grandma that she'd split the seams by just dipping a toe into them.

"Wait, Grandma." Jenn resisted, and her grandmother stopped to face her on the sidewalk. "What's going on?"

"Just come with me—"

"No." Jenn said the word as forcefully as she could, more forcefully than she'd ever said anything to Grandma before. She wasn't the same Jenn, who would meekly allow others to dictate her life. "Tell me what's going on. I needed that job for more than one reason."

Grandma's face registered annoyance but also a grudging respect. "Very well. I wanted to tell you in the comfort of my office, but in the middle of Japantown is fine, too."

Jenn ignored her acerbic tone and stood her ground, crossing her arms.

"Your small business loan was approved."

"Grandma! I told you to withdraw it. What am I going to do with it?"

"Start your own business, of course," she snapped as if Jenn were a simpleton.

Jenn blinked at her in annoyed disbelief. "With Mom the way she is?"

"Your own business lets you set your own hours so you can take care of her."

"Sure I can take care of her. With what money?"

Grandma then smiled. A triumphant smile that had Jenn a little frightened, to be honest. "You now have a monthly stipend."

"That's news to me. Since when?"

"Since today. The first month's check is at the bank."

"And who is my mysterious benefactor? Santa Claus?" Jenn really hoped it wasn't Grandma. Or Venus. While she knew they only did it out of love, she hated the feeling of being a charity case. It made her feel like she was less of a person.

"Mr. and Mrs. Yip."

It took her a second to register the names. "As in, Brad Yip's parents?"

Grandma nodded grandly. She could have been the queen granting everyone a tax break.

"Why in the world are they giving me a stipend?"

"As compensation for taking care of their family goat, Pookie."

"What? Pookie? How did you get them to do that?"

"They have a brother in considerable debt … to the bank."

Jenn was beginning to see the threads of Grandma's weaving as they formed her web.

"They were so surprised to hear that when Brad gave you Pookie to take care of, he hadn't offered any form of compensation. They were very embarrassed. I suggested a sum that would be adequate for all the work you're doing or that would enable you to stable Pookie at a farm." She named an absurd amount that had Jenn gasping.

"Grandma!" She stopped short of accusing her grandparent of extortion in the middle of the busy street.

"I consider it adequate," she replied. "Especially in light of their son's behavior to you."

"Brad?"

Grandma's eyes softened then. "Jenn, I didn't remember that incident until you confronted him at the party, or else I would never have allowed him to be invited."

The words draped over her, warming her like the softest down. "Thank you."

"So. Shall we?" She gestured to her waiting car.

"Yes." She followed her Grandma, joyous at being sprung from her teriyaki-coated prison.

They snuck into church like a foursome of thieves.

Except thieves wouldn't have stalked into the sanctuary on Venus's three-inch-high designer heels—which she insisted were shorter than what she used to wear—or tripped over her own shoes like Lex, or exaggeratedly tiptoed in like Trish.

Jenn followed a few feet behind, unsure if she really wanted to sit next to them and announce to all and sundry that she claimed them as acquaintances.

Then again, it was the fault of all four of them. They wouldn't have been late to Sunday service if Trish hadn't insisted they all drive together, and if Lex hadn't been as late as she always was, and if NASCAR-racer Venus hadn't kept nagging Jenn about how slow she was driving, which of course made Jenn drive even more carefully just to be perverse.

Normally they didn't all go to church together, but for the first weekend in a long time, Aiden, Spencer, and Drake were all out of town, and the four cousins had elected to go to church together and then have lunch and go to a chick flick at the theater.

Venus found them a seat by zeroing in on a pew taken up by several lounging teenage boys and ordering them to "move over." They complied like peons in a boardroom, squeezing their lanky frames together so the four cousins could sit without spilling into each others' laps.

Trish knocked elbows with Jenn, which made her clench her teeth to keep from yelping. She happened to glance to the side as she rubbed her stinging elbow, and that's when she saw it.

The polar ice caps must have melted because a few rows down and across the aisle from her, sitting in a pew, was the last person she would have ever expected to see in church.

Grandma Sakai.

Jenn backhanded Trish's arm, not taking her eyes off Grandma, just in case she dissolved.

"What?" Trish said.

Jenn pointed to Grandma.

Trish sucked in air so fast she started coughing.

Jenn wasn't hallucinating. That really was Grandma.

Trish slapped Lex while still coughing.

"Will you keep it d—" Lex's sentence was swallowed by her shock as she saw Grandma. She slapped Venus, sitting next to her.

"Toddlers would behave better than you three. What is it?" she whispered.

All three cousins pointed fingers at Grandma, who was still oblivious to their shock and amazement.

"Oh. Is that all?"

"What do you mean, *'Is that all?'*" Lex hissed.

Venus shrugged. "Mrs. Matsumoto and Grandma have been coming to church for several weeks now."

"And you didn't tell us?" Trish's whisper was sharp and incredulous.

"Shut up, you're disrupting the service." Venus faced forward and ignored their astounded looks.

Jenn had known Grandma had patched things up with her good friend Mrs. Matsumoto, who happened to be a very outspoken Christian, after the two of them had argued a year ago. When they became friends again—it really reminded Jenn of a high school drama, the whole thing had been so silly—Mrs. Matsumoto had managed to get Grandma to go to some church-sponsored senior group meetings. But Jenn hadn't known she'd somehow managed to get Grandma to go to church.

Then again, now that Lex and Aiden were married (by elopement, no less), Lex no longer came to this church, instead going to Aiden's. Jenn had also been going to Valley Bible Church with Lex, Aiden, Trish, and Spenser, and only Venus came to Santa Clara Church because she and Drake worked with the youth group on Saturday nights. So if Grandma and Mrs. Matsumoto were coming here, only Venus would have known.

During announcements, Venus wrote in her program and passed it to the three cousins, who hunched over Trish to read it.

Mrs. Matsumoto & Grandma have become friends w/ Mrs. Cathcart, who runs Sunday school pgrm. She invited them to senior group that meets here after church. They've been coming for 2 months.

Two months? The three cousins hadn't known that their staunchly Buddhist, verbally anti-Christian Grandma had been going to Venus's church for two months?

Well, no, Jenn couldn't say Grandma had been as snidely anti-Christian in the past half year, not since she and Mrs. Matsumoto were back to being BFFs. When they had broken up, Grandma had been a bit insulting to Lex and Trish about their faith, but she hadn't said anything about the cousins' faith in the past few months, to be honest.

The service dragged on forever. Jenn was dying to go up to Grandma. But really, what would she say? "Hi, grandma, funny seeing you here, so have you become a Christian yet?"

Well, she'd think of something. The pastor was certainly talking an awfully long—

At that moment, she noticed the table standing to the side near the front of the sanctuary. Faux-silver, deep-rimmed plates stood stacked on top of each other.

Just when she thought the service would be wrapping up … nope. It was the weekend for the church's quarterly communion. She'd have to wait an extra fifteen minutes to talk to Grandma.

The pastor started the communion, clarifying that all Christians were encouraged to take communion, even if they weren't members of this church, but that they asked nonbelievers to abstain.

The ushers passed some shallow-rimmed plates, each containing broken pieces of bread. While waiting, Jenn watched idly as people took their bread.

The plate got to Grandma, and Jenn was hardly paying attention until it seemed that Grandma dipped her hand in the plate.

What?

Jenn stared hard at her, but it was difficult to tell if she'd taken a piece of bread or not. She shook Trish's arm. "Did you see that?"

"See what?"

"Grandma."

"Grandma what?"

Maybe Jenn had imagined it.

The pastor had asked everyone to hold their pieces of bread so they could take them all together to signify their unity as the body of Christ.

Jenn, feeling guilty, didn't really pay attention to him because she was watching Grandma like a hawk. But she didn't have a good angle—she was further up the aisle as opposed to directly across from her—and when they raised their hands to their mouths to take the bread, she couldn't be sure Grandma had eaten anything.

Had she taken a piece of bread? Jenn's heart picked up speed as the ushers then passed around the deep-rimmed plates, which each contained tiny plastic cups of grape juice.

When the plate got to Grandma, she didn't even hesitate. Very matter-of-factly, she took a cup.

Jenn's entire body suddenly jolted as if she'd been hit by lightning. Beside Jenn, Trish yelped softly. Venus shushed them but then caught sight of Grandma, whose outside hand clearly held a cup of juice. An intense look settled on Venus's face.

"Seriously?" Lex whispered. "Seriously?"

"You didn't know this?" Jenn asked Venus, who shook her head.

Grandma. A Christian.

The thought made her want to laugh. To cry. To shout.

But then her heart plummeted back to earth. Maybe Grandma was only taking the cup so she wouldn't look weird to not be taking it in front of everybody.

But Mrs. Matsumoto, sitting next to Grandma, wouldn't have let her do that. And Mrs. Matsumoto looked rather complacent as she sat there.

"Jenn." Trish nudged her.

She looked down at the plate of grape juice cups. Oh, right. Communion. She took a cup.

The pastor had asked people to take the cup as they felt led, to signify each person's individual commitment to Christ. Well, it was kind of a no-brainer what she wanted to talk to God about. She closed her eyes.

Whoa. God. How could I ever think something was too big for You?

Hadn't the past week taught her that? Being rescued by Grandma, receiving her first check from the Yips only seven days after getting the news about Mom? (Granted, that had been a slightly stressful seven days.)

And now this. Completely unexpected but utterly amazing, filled with the grace and power of God. Of all her relatives, she would never have imagined that hard-nosed businesswoman and matriarch Grandma Sakai would turn from her lifetime of faithfulness to Buddha to Jesus Christ.

Jenn shivered. It was too much for her to even comprehend. God was so much bigger than she'd ever imagined.

Jenn noticed movement next to her. Trish was standing with everyone else for the final song and the benediction.

Jenn hastily slammed back the grape juice and scrambled to her feet.

As soon as the worship leader dismissed them, Jenn shot out of her seat and zeroed in on Grandma. "Hi, Grandma!"

Unfortunately, her exuberance made her spit a little on Grandma's linen suit. She winced as heat crept up her neck to engulf her ears. "Sorry about that."

Her three cousins had followed and stood around her now, making her feel a little less like a dork as they greeted Grandma.

She eyed them all, face looking exactly like normal. "You're blocking the aisle."

The ordinariness of it all made Jenn wonder if she mistook what had happened. She exchanged a puzzled look with Lex, but they stood aside so she and Mrs. Matsumoto could exit the pew.

The cousins followed them into the social hall, where tea and coffee were set out on a table. "Lex," Grandma said, "could you please get me some tea?"

"Sure, Grandma."

As soon as she was gone, Grandma turned to Trish. "Oh, I forgot. Could you get Mrs. Matsumoto some tea, too?"

Trish's face registered surprise, but she went.

"And Venus—"

"I'm disappearing, Grandma." Venus turned to Mrs. Matsumoto. "I think Mrs. Cathcart brought in a box of doughnuts to serve with the coffee. Do you want to come with me to the kitchen to help me cut them up?"

When the two of them were gone, Grandma turned to Jenn, who was a bit alarmed at this impromptu meeting. "Um … I guess you wanted to talk to me alone?"

"Mrs. Matsumoto suggested I talk to you."

"Is she okay?"

"She's fine." Grandma waved the question away, but then paused as if gathering her thoughts. "I was talking to her last week, right after we found out about your mom. I told her something that she suggested you might like to hear from me."

Jenn was completely perplexed. This was not Grandma. This was someone who looked like Grandma but who had gone all touchy-feely-emo on her.

"Jenn, I have always thought of you as the good girl. Everyone in the family took advantage of you, but you were always helpful, you were always gentle, you were always nurturing. And you always mentioned Jesus and pointed to your faith."

Really? Jenn didn't think she talked as much about her faith as Trish did (well, except for those few months Trish was dating that weird artist guy, not going to church, and getting into all kinds of trouble, including conceiving Elyssa). Jenn had always thought she was singularly quiet about her faith.

"I was very glad when you quit your job to start your catering business."

"You were?" Jenn chewed her lip. "At the time, I thought you might be upset at me, like Mom and all the aunties."

"No, I was very pleased. Because for once in your life, you were showing some backbone."

That made sense. Jenn had once told Venus that Grandma actually got along best with her because of their similar determined personalities, which would explain why Grandma was pleased about Jenn's bid for independence.

"But when I saw that you were willing to give up your dreams to work for Aunty for your mom's sake, when I saw what you were willing to do, it suddenly made sense to me why you'd been such a doormat before."

"Gee. Thanks, Grandma."

Grandma ignored her sarcasm and reached up to touch her cheek. "You helped your family members without complaining because of your faith. You were willing to work for Aunty Aikiko because of your love for your mom and because of your faith. Your faith made you a better person."

Jenn squirmed. "I don't think I'm a *better* person, Grandma."

She pinched Jenn's cheek lightly. "Don't argue with me. You are. I had been going to church with Mrs. Matsumoto for a few weeks, so I knew what that 'something' in you was."

Jenn had "something" in her? She'd always felt so un-something. So ordinary. So … Jenn.

"Jenn, you are the reason I went to see the pastor to become a Christian. I wanted you to know that." Her hand fell away from Jenn's face, and there was a serenity in the intelligent eyes that she hadn't seen before.

Grandma was still Grandma. She hadn't suddenly turned into another Mrs. Matsumoto with her fervent, out-loud prayers every time she felt the Spirit move, her computer-like memory for Bible verses, and her favorite quote, "Praise God!"

No, Grandma was still reserved, sharp as a whip, and the reigning matriarch of the Sakai family. But she had a softer understanding in her eyes that Jenn recognized on a deep, almost subconscious level.

God had put that there. God had used Jenn, and she hadn't even known it.

She exhaled long and deep. She was humbled and honored.

Jenn's cell phone vibrated against her body where her purse, slung over her shoulder, rested against her ribcage. At the same moment, Trish approached with Grandma's tea. Lex had apparently seen that Grandma wanted to talk to Jenn and was trying to detain Trish, but Trish swatted aside her grasping hand and said, "No, Grandma said she wanted tea, lemme go, what are you doing?"

"Thank you, Trish." Grandma took the tea and ended her conversation with Jenn. So Jenn dug out her phone and checked the caller ID.

Edward.

Grandma was in good hands with Trish and Lex, right? "Hello?"

"Hi, gorgeous."

There was that melty chocolate lava cake feeling in her ribcage again. "H-hi."

"I need to talk to you. I have a, um ... business proposition for you."

"Oh." How dare he call her gorgeous and then want to talk about business?

"And, uh ... I've missed you." His voice hit a low note that vibrated in the pit of her stomach.

He was forgiven. "I'm cooking lunch for my family today. Want to join us?"

"Sure. I'll even bring a present for Pookie."

His present was a real feeding trough, which he'd dug out of his family's storage barn. "It's an old one of Aunty Lorena's." He presented it to the goat like Vanna White.

Jenn giggled. "I fed her this morning, so I'll use it when I feed her tonight." She made to move back into the house and thought she saw movement at the edge of the back door into the house.

But then Edward detained her with a hand on her arm. "Wait. I need to talk to you."

"I need to start making lunch."

Through the open kitchen window, someone shouted, "No, she doesn't!" It sounded suspiciously like Trish. Or Lex. They sounded alike.

Jenn closed her eyes and set her teeth, but she still felt the sunburn firing up her neck to her ears. She whirled around to put her back to the prying eyes inside the house and sighed as she looked up at Edward. "Sorry."

His eyes had crinkled. "You've met my family. They wouldn't be trying to hide behind the edge of the door. They'd be pushing each other for front-row seating."

She would be willing to bet Venus was in the upstairs bedroom with a pair of binoculars and some high-tech microphone she got from work. Jenn cleared her throat. "You needed to tell me something?"

"I know you were going to give up your catering business because of your mom's treatments. But what about your own restaurant?"

Her breath caught. That would be a dream, but ... "I don't have the money for something like that."

"Well, it wouldn't quite be your own restaurant ... yet. But Castillo Winery has a bed and breakfast that's been doing very well for the past several years. My uncle has tossed around the idea of opening a restaurant there since we already have a large dining area and the kitchen all set up, but none of the family wants to undertake it. So I mentioned you."

Jenn's heartbeat ramped up. Did he really mean it? Her own restaurant? "You talked to your uncle about me?"

"You'd technically be hired by the winery, so you'd have a salary and insurance—which I thought you might not mind because of your mom."

She absolutely didn't mind at all.

"But my uncle is willing to give you free rein in the kitchen, so it would almost be like having your own restaurant."

Her own restaurant. "I can make anything?"

"Anything."

"I can bring my own staff?" They'd be ecstatic to work with her in a restaurant.

"Sure."

Her joy zapped out of her arms like electricity, and she flung them around Edward's neck. "Oh, yes! Thank you thank you thank you!"

"Did he propose?" came a shocked whisper from behind her. It sounded like Mrs. Matsumoto.

"No!" Jenn and Edward both yelled for the benefit of their eavesdroppers.

"I wish he'd kiss her" came from the house. That sounded like Grandma.

And so he did.

His mouth moved over hers with the freshness of spring, the promise of new beginnings, not just for her restaurant, but also for them. His scent of verbena and thyme swirled around her, and his hands tightened at the base of her spine, drawing her closer to him.

She leaned into his body, tightening her arms around his neck, and he deepened the kiss. Her skin felt alive and vibrant, because this was Edward, and he wasn't just her *friend*.

He drew his head back, looking down at her with dark eyes a little glazed, like the glossy shell of a chocolate truffle.

"I liked that," she breathed. "I'd like some more."

But as his head descended again, his face suddenly lurched forward, knocking her in the nose. "What—?" He twisted around to look behind him.

Pookie stood there, staring up at them.

"Pookie! You poked him! Bad Pookie!" Jenn said.

Edward turned back to her, his arms wrapping around her again as he murmured in her ear, "I really think you need to rename that goat."

AUTHOR'S NOTE

FOR MOST OF my books, I have a particular album I listen to that inspires me. For this book, it was *Every Time I Breathe* by Big Daddy Weave: **http://tinyurl.com/4prs8rl**.

The song. "Let It Rise" can be found on iTunes here: **http://tinyurl.com/yeavpsa**. I hope the song inspires you to worship with abandon the way it does for Trish and for me.

The song Trish sings in the park is "Every Time I Breathe": **http://tinyurl.com/4oh2v9l**. The lyrics always speak to my heart and help me focus on Jesus and feel His presence.

The Malaysian basil is completely fictional, although some of you will recognize it—and the dermatologist researcher—from my romantic suspense novel *Formula for Danger.*

WinePressPublishing
Great Books, Defined.

To order additional copies of this book call:
1-877-421-READ (7323)
or please visit our website at
www.WinePressbooks.com

If you enjoyed this quality custom-published book,
drop by our website for more books and information.

www.winepresspublishing.com
"Your partner in custom publishing."

CPSIA information can be obtained at www.ICGtesting.com
Printed in the USA
LVOW051005280712

291960LV00002B/7/P